Endless Beginnings
Carl Messinger

Copyright © 2024 Carl Messinger

All rights reserved. No part of this book may be reproduced or transmitted in any form or by any means, electronic or mechanical, including photocopying, recording or by any information storage and retrieval system without permission in writing from the publisher.

JKL Publishing—Scottsdale, AZ
ISBN: 979-8-218-45428-9
Library of Congress Control Number: 2024913980
Title: *Endless Beginnings*
Author: Carl Messinger
Digital distribution | 2024
Paperback | 2024

This is a work of fiction. The characters, names, incidents, places, and dialogue are products of the author's imagination, and are not to be construed as real.

Published in the United States by New Book Authors Publishing

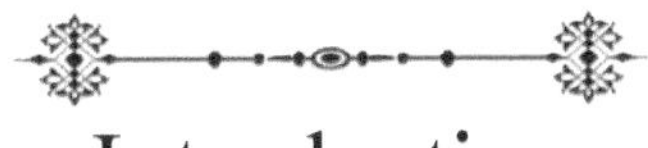

Introduction

Hi, my name is Carl, and I am a procrastinator. Yep, that's what I am, a procrastinator. I was born that way, two weeks after my scheduled birth date. Just the way it was. And it has followed me all through life, sometimes resulting in good things, like delaying my soldiers from storming across a field which immediately came under misdirected artillery fire, to delaying a phone call which changed my life forever. It is what happens when one is a procrastinator.

But despite this handicap, this is the third book of the trilogy I promised myself years ago that I would write. Oh, I had done some writing before, some travel articles, some theater reviews, but not anything like this. This was different. This was a project that was going to take years, many years, several years, all years during which my procrastination could take hold. But it didn't.

And why do I tell you this? Simply because there are people out there with wonderful ideas, creative thoughts, imaginations which exceed the boundaries of what we know and think, and, for whatever reason, they refuse to let those ideas, those thoughts, those imaginations escape from the inside to the outside. They also are procrastinators. Like me, they start a project and halfway through put it aside, never to be completed. It sits there, dormant, unfinished, languishing in limbo waiting to be released. But for some reason, we, you, are afraid to let it out.

Well, let me tell you. Letting it out is the Lexar of the gods. It overcomes the fear, it overcomes the anxiety, and it overcomes the concern of acceptance. It is the panacea of one's soul. It is the "I did it" moment when all else falls by the wayside. It is the beginning and the realization that "I did it once, I can do it again." It is the opening of new doors to the future. It is you as only you can be.

So, I dedicate this work to those who are struggling to do their own work in the hope that the words above give you a little strength to strive and reach your goal. To overcome the obstacles which stand in your way, and at the end, to say "I did it."

Chapter One

The aromatic smell of brewed coffee wafted across the small divide between the kitchen and the bedroom as it headed toward and out the open window seeking vast spaces to search and explore. Natalie sniffed the strong smell, her eyes still shut as the evening's activities delivered its last effects. With what seemed like her final bit of strength, her arms escaped from the confines of the warm blanket and reached to grasp—nothing. For nothing was there and she opened her eyes to reveal the slow revolving of the ceiling fan and a faint light in the kitchen area.

She forced herself to lean forward, resting her weight on her elbows and peered into the kitchen, seeing only a figure sitting at the table sipping a cup of the same coffee she smelled. Looking around the surroundings, she recognized her bedroom, the nightstand with the clock, the tiny table upon which rested her purse and several other familiar objects all of which eased her feelings of wonderment where she was and calmed the nerves. With a little trepidation, she spoke.

"Chris, is that you?"

The silent figure in the kitchen turned around with a smile on his face. "Yes," he said, with a questioning glance. "Look who finally got up."

Natalie slowly pushed the covers aside, then quickly covered herself up again, afraid of what she would expose with the unveiling. A quick inspection revealed a crumpled skirt still worn and a wrinkled bra covering her upper body. Satisfied with the results, she swung her legs out from under the covers and over the side of the bed, resting her feet on the floor and raising her head to the level of "oh my God" before lowering them to her open palms and shutting her eyes.

"Are you all right?" asked Chris.

"I'm fine, just as soon as I get off this cloud and find something solid to stand on."

Chris laughed, got up, and walked over to the bed, sitting down alongside her. "A little foggy head this morning, eh?" he asked with a little grin in his voice.

"I don't know," she said, "I'll tell you when I find it."

He chuckled a little and offered her some coffee. She stood up and leaned on his shoulder. They carefully moved to the kitchen table and sat down gingerly.

"What happened last night? I don't remember much."

"Well, don't quite know where to start," said Chris. "After the ceremony, you, Stick and John went over to Beach Bum's. Tiny was there waiting for you and had your table readied for a party. Wine was in place as well as some food and congratulation cards. People were excited to be there and the atmosphere was great. I arrived about an hour after you guys, having taken care of the Honor Guard as thanks for their contribution and made sure the Colonel and Captain knew the Governor would be extending his thanks. In any event, the party continued for a while and you really liked the wine! After the third glass, there appeared to be no pain at all.

"Half-way through the fourth glass, your head began to sag and well-meant words were repeated and slurred. That's when we all decided it was time enough to end the festivities and I should take you back to the cottage. And so I did.

"I figured you could hold onto my arm and we would walk to the cottage and get settled. All was going well, though there were a few mis-steps until you sagged and wanted to sit on the ground to rest for a minute. Well, that didn't last long as you rolled over and looked like sleep was around the corner. In any event, I picked you up and put you over my shoulder and off we went. In all honestly, it was not easy as I had had my share of booze, but we made it. I laid you on the bed and wondered what to do next.

"Several thoughts came to mind but I quickly, OK, not so quickly, discarded them. In any event, I did remove your blouse, thinking that would make you a little more comfortable but left everything else on. You may have to make a dry cleaners run for the skirt, by the way. I slid you under the covers, made sure the pillow was under your head, opened the window a little to let some fresh air in, covered you up, kissed your forehead, and turned out the light.

"As for me," Chris continued, "I found a couple of extra blankets in the closet, stole the second pillow from your bed, and made myself comfortable on the couch. Not the most desired spot but suitable for one night. Got up this morning and made some coffee. That's when you woke up. Now that you are awake and semi-functioning, I can leave as I have some work to do. Are you OK with that?"

Natalie fidgeted for a minute. "Sure, I can handle that. And Chris, thank you for taking care of me last night. Not sure why the need arose. I know it was an emotional event for me, recognizing the man who saved my father's life and gave me the opportunity to get to know him. It was like celebrating a birth. I was happy for Stick, and was happy for Dad, knowing he would have liked to thank Stick himself. I owe you one, Sir. I won't forget."

"Now you need to get about your business while I figure out what to do next."

Chris stood and emptied his cup into the sink. "There's more coffee in the pot if you want some. I would take it easy today, just rest up, recuperate, and be ready for tomorrow. The early part of the week is always the worst. I'll call you later to make sure all is OK and we'll talk about dinner during the week."

Natalie stood up and moved to Chris, hugging him close and feeling the connection between them. "You take care, dear. Looking forward to your call."

Chris walked out the cottage toward his car. Natalie looked around the kitchen, sighed, turned off the coffee pot, and with a sigh of resolution, crawled back into bed.

The sun rose and a new day begun.

Chapter Two

There's something about waking up twice in one day. It's like you snuck away from the cares of the world, covered yourself with pleasant dreams, experienced the warm sun on a snow-covered iceberg, and stole a few hours of agonizing life, only to awake to a different day, a different time, and sometimes even a different planet. Not because of the second wakeup, but because of the wonderful nap which preceded it. For naps are like pennies from heaven. And Natalie had just received a pocket full, as she opened her eyes.

Nothing had changed in the cottage. Oh well, the coffee had gotten cold but that was easily remedied. Natalie tested out her extremities and laughed as each one seemed to function as usual. And funny, all the blurred objects which had greeted her earlier had used the nap time to adjust their sight and they now appeared sharp and clear in their appointed places.

Natalie swung her legs over the bed and sat upright, taking in the bright sunshine peeking around the shade and absorbing the light breeze filtering through the window. A quick glance at the clock brought her up quickly. It was two o'clock in the afternoon, the day almost gone and she still had to drive home on the Sunday afternoon.

Gingerly testing her limbs, she stood up straight and paddled, rather than walk, to the kitchen area, heading straight to the coffee. With a quick twist, she turned on the pot and sat down, not wanting to overdue the strain of walking. The pot eventually buzzed, and she welcomed the hot liquid across her tongue and down her throat.

"Nectar of the Gods," she thought as a to-do list began to appear. Another sip and she started to attack the list and thirty minutes later, showered and dressed, she was ready to leave.

"Hello, Natalie," said Irma, the proprietor of the White Horse Inn and desk clerk. "Glad you are feeling better. Chris stopped by before leaving and said to let you sleep. Said you needed it. Hopefully it worked."

"Morning, ah, afternoon Irma. Thanks for letting me get past the hurt. All is well and I'm heading north. Tomorrow is a work day and need to be ready for that. Have a good week and I'll tell your sister you said hi."

"OK," said Irma. "Drive carefully and tell Margaret to call me, I have some gossip to share."

Natalie chuckled as she hung up. Irma and Margaret were good friends and she enjoyed them both. With Margaret being her assistant and Irma owning the cottages down at the shore, she always had a place to stay and get away from the crowds and noise of the airport.

Natalie drove her car through the back streets till reaching the main highway. Turning right, she eased into the traffic and settled into the two, two and a half drive to Newark and her homestead apartment. Nothing special but it was home.

The drive provided Natalie with the opportunity to think about the past, her life, what she had done, what she hadn't done, where she was and perhaps more importantly, where she was going. The latter was somewhat of a blur, as like spreading limbs from a tree, it was unclear which one was the lead, which one to follow. Only time could tell that.

Her thoughts began to wander, following a path that seemed to take her nowhere, but everywhere. she thought about her life as a little girl, how she grew up in the small mid-western town, devoid of a father, and relying on her grandfather to provide her fatherly advice. The only problem with that was he was from the Old Country, loved the Old Country, and wanted to live as though he was still in the Old Country. But this was America. Things were different, times were different and adjustment was the word of the day. He had settled in a small village mostly made up of German immigrants, all of whom wanted to maintain the ways of the Old Country. Working various jobs until he saved enough money, he opened a small gasthaus, like the one back home, and even named it zum Ross II, after his deceased wife's favorite flower, her grandmother whom she had never met. It flourished and eventually became the social hub of the village. Her mother, Ingrid, worked at the restaurant between stints cleaning houses and eventually took over when her father was unable to continue due to age.

And then I came along, thought Natalie, making it even a little more difficult. Ingrid had explained to the neighbors that her husband had died during the Berlin Blockade, and that event, and her father's concern about a third war, led them to immigrant to America. That explanation seemed to quell any questions. Life went on, and the next few years were a blur in young Natalie's mind.

Adolescence went along as normal, as if any adolescence seems normal to the one experiencing it. School came and went, year after year. Seemed like the same thing. Most of the events during that time never left an impression, except one. And that yearly one hurt. The Father and Daughter dance. It happened every year and every year Natalie felt left out.

Her grandfather would take her when she was younger and it raised no questions. But as she grew older and entered high school, students would begin to question her either for showing up with her grandfather, or not showing up at all after his passing. And while she explained to her friends what she thought was the truth, it never seemed like it was enough or them, or even her. She even questioned her mom as to what her dad was like, only to receive vague answers, alluding to a special time in her life that she remembered but couldn't repeat.

Despite several attempts at dating, her mother never seemed satisfied with the results. Her mind appeared to be elsewhere.

Eventually the letter came, accepting her to college. Her mother was not happy because the college she wanted to attend was on the East coast. To Natalie, it was heaven-sent, a chance to see the real world and a chance to enter the business environment she yearned for. With New York just across the river, the college in New Jersey was perfect. Not quite in the "City" but close enough to be accessible. Four years later and an intern stint at Johnson and Johnson she answered an ad from Condor Airlines, was accepted, and now, as fate would have it, led it.

The exit off the highway almost passed by, the thoughts Natalie was going through clouding the task at hand. But reality quickly resumed and she guided the vehicle to its intended destination, the little two-story house she called home, and had since first starting at Condor. The car pulled smoothly onto the driveway and quietly moved to the back of the house. Natalie got out, grabbed her bag from the back seat and walked to the stairs leading to her upstairs apartment. In a moment of intellectual impression, she envisioned the stairs as her escalator from intern to CEO.

She laughed as she climbed the stairs, carrying her bag as it clanked against the steps. "So much for CEO," she thought with a chuckle.

The apartment was just as she left it, neat and tidy. She unpacked, put things away and got ready to resume the horizontal position for the night. It was only then that she noticed the blinking red light on her phone, an indication that someone had called and left a message. No telling how long it had been beckoning, she walked over to the nightstand and stared at the pleading light. "Not tonight," she murmured, picking up the receiver and putting it back down. "Tomorrow is soon enough."

The sheets were nice and cool as the weekend faded and another round of duties began.

Chapter Three

"She just walked in," Margaret said into the phone as Natalie entered the front door and started up the stairs. "I'll tell her you want to talk with her."

"Morning, Margaret. Day starting early? Who were you talking to?"

"John. He needs to talk to you. He's on the way."

"Send him in. I need a cup of coffee."

Before Natalie had even gotten halfway to her desk, John was knocking on her office door, breathing heavily as a result of rushing up the stairs. She looked at him in a quizzical manner, wondering what prompted this. "What's going on?"

John stopped midway to her desk, shuffled some papers, and looked at her seriously. "Natalie, you want the good news or the bad news first?"

"Well, from the sound of your voice, there isn't much good news, but let's hear what you have."

John cleared his throat, checked his papers again, and looked up. He looked at Natalie and said, "Reports are that everyone is OK, there have been no injuries or deaths."

Natalie's face went pale, as she realized this was the good news. If this was the good news, what was the bad news, she wondered.

"OK, let's have the bad news. What's going on?"

John again glanced at his papers and stammered. "According to information from Zink, one of our aircraft has been hijacked and being held at Frankfurt Airport waiting to move onward to an, so far, unknown destination. Operations there are trying to hold up the plane's departure until plans can be made to take control of it again. He's working with both civilian and military authorities to format a plan to safeguard all concerned, the plane, the cargo, and the crew. We have been in constant touch since this happened and are providing all the support we can."

Natalie thought for a minute. "Zink, who is Zink."

John replied, "Zink, Dieter Zink, European Operations Director whose office is at Frankfurt. He is relatively new."

"Right," said Natalie, "I know him by his first name so did not recognize the name Zink. I remember talking with him before bringing him on board. Seemed like a competent manager at the time. We shall see."

"How did this happen, John?"

"Well, reports indicate that three men dressed in ground-crew attire stormed the main cabin door when the co-pilot opened it to allow customs and immigration officials to board. The intruders forced the crew into the cockpit and shut and locked the cabin door, preventing anyone else from entering. They forced the pilot to contact ground control and explain what happened, including the fact that all crew members were all right. That was a good thing for Pat to do."

"Yes, that was a good thing and a relief for him to do that," sighed Natalie.

"She," said John.

"She?"

"She, Patricia McHenry, retired Air Force pilot with hundreds of flight hours in all types of planes. She is a pro. In fact, the whole crew are women."

Natalie paused and thought for a minute. "OK, listen carefully, there is one thing I want you and Zink to understand. The safety and well-being of the crew come first, before anything else. While the plane and cargo are important, insurance can take care of most of the damage there. But they come after the crew. I want that understood by everyone involved. The crew must be protected and saved."

There was no misunderstanding where Natalie stood on the safety of the crew. If there was any doubt, it was erased with the next comment.

"How soon can we get over there?"

***

Two hours later Natalie abruptly stood up behind her desk, walked resolutely out the office door, past Margaret, "Hold my calls. Except Chris. If he calls, tell him I will call him later," and down the stairs. She turned quickly and stepped through the door marked "Operations Directorate," stopping short of the receptionist's desk

9

inside. Looking around at the empty offices of the Director and Deputy Director, she extended her arms, palms up, shrugged her shoulders as if to say "where is everybody?"

The receptionist politely stood up and pointed to the solitary door on the opposite wall. "In the control room," she said.

Natalie walked over to the door, opened it, and stepped into an entirely new world. Scattered round the room in some sort of logical position which was not readily apparent were desks with monitors manned by technicians watching over the workings of Condor airlines throughout the world. Everyone seemed engrossed in their individual tasks, unaware of others around, going about their work to in a professional fashion, keeping the airline on or ahead of schedule. Only one such station seemed to stand out.

In the far corner was a stand-alone, single monitoring station. A technician sat in front of the screen and standing behind him were Dick, the Director of Operations, and John, his deputy and son of Stick. A few others stood behind them, basically listening to what was happening and ready to fulfill any orders from the two men. Natalie walked up behind them and stood quietly and listened before coughing and speaking.

Before the first words were out of her mouth, John turned around and with his finger pressed against his lips, shushed the intrusion. Realizing it was Natalie, he broke away from the group and motioned her to follow him away from the station.

"OK," she said. "What is going on?"

"We're talking with the pilot of the hijacked plane, Pat McHenry. She's still on the plane."

"Can't the hijackers hear her," asked Natalie.

"We have a special, secure transmission frequency, actually most of our planes have it, which allows the pilot to talk with operations here without revealing it to anyone on the plane or even the FAA control functions. All airlines are assigned an emergency frequency, such as this one, to communicate directly with the company on matters which do not include the FAA. We installed a small radio transmitter under the pilot's seat with a switch on the seat between the pilot and the fuselage of the plane, enabling the pilot to quietly communicate with us here without alerting unwanted personnel. It is rarely used, but is coming in handy in this case. Let's go back and listen."

"—And so, we are doing all right as of now," said the voice over the speaker. "Dieter has been keeping us fed and hydrated with food and water and keeping us up to date as to what is going on outside. Oops, gotta go."

"What is going on with the plane? When is it scheduled to depart, and where is it going?"

"Well," said John, "Dieter has done a good job in delaying its departure, first with the refueling effort, seems like it was the last one in line, and second with the required safety check, which revealed chips in the number four engine fan. A secondary inspection is being conducted as it appears FOD damaged the fans. Perhaps it was an errant wrench or other mysterious object causing the damage. In any event, some mechanic deserves a talking to— and probably a bonus. In any event, the engine will have to be repaired or replaced which will take at least a day. That gives us a little time."

"Speaking of time," continued John, "we have a plane departing for Frankfurt at 2150 hours, getting in around 7 in the morning. I have told them to expect passengers, how many I don't know. Do you know who is going, besides you and I?"

"Plan on 5 or 6 people to be on the safe side. Don't know who they will be but we will figure it out. You have any suggestions?"

John paused for a minute. "Stick," he said.

"Why?" was the curt response.

"He knows the airplane. He worked for Lockheed when it manufactured the C-141. The hijacked plane is a commercially modified C-141. Stick knows it backwards and forwards and can be valuable in helping gain entrance if that is necessary. He may not be young and up to date on everything, but he is a fountain of knowledge concerning older things. He should be there to help."

Natalie thought for a minute. "OK," she concurred. "Add him to the list. There will be others but plan for no more than six total. We'll get together this afternoon and determine who exactly that six will be."

"I'll be in my office. Don't keep me wondering what is going on for so long. I need to know."

John nodded in agreement and turned to walk back to the monitoring station. Natalie knew the situation was in as good of hands as possible and slowly walked back to her office. As CEO, there were a myriad of other items to handle.

"Margaret, hold the phone again. I have an important call to make."

Natalie picked up the desk phone and called Chris's private line. He answered on the first ring.

"What is going on? I heard the news this morning about a plane being hijacked in Frankfurt and it sounded like one of yours. Is that the case?"

"It is," said Natalie. "Terrorists have taken over the plane and threatened to blow it up, along with the crew, unless they are flown to, who knows where. I am flying over there this evening on one of our planes to see how I can help."

"I want you to come with me."

Chris balked at his reply. "I don't know if I can do that. There is a lot of things going on now, and I need to be here for them."

"Chris, I need you there. You have experience with dealing with people and negotiating compromises that I don't. I need your help," she asked again.

"I don't know if the Governor will let me go. He relies heavily on me."

"Chris, let me put it this way. Condor Airlines is a New Jersey corporation. The three-person crew, all females, are all New Jersey residents and vote in New Jersey. Thousands of employees of Condor reside and vote in New Jersey. Your boss, the Governor of New Jersey, is so concerned about the safety of the New Jersey crew, and the financial loss that Condor would sustain should anything happened to the aircraft, that he is sending his most senior representative, his most trusted and most experienced advisor, as his personal representative to help wherever possible and defuse the situation, bringing home the New Jersey residents which represents his Constitutional duty as Governor of New Jersey. He is doing his sworn duty."

"And Chris," she said with a sigh, "I want you with me."

A pause filled the miles between them. It seemed like an eternity till the voice on the other end spoke. "I'll talk with the Governor. Be right back."

It seemed like each second took at minute, and each minute took an hour, until finally the voice came on the line.

"What time should I be at the airport?"

A smile suddenly appeared on her face, erasing all the pent-up worries and concerns. "Meet me at the airport. John and Stick are going also and we can discuss how to approach this thing. Tell the Governor 'Thank You' from me. He has my vote."

"Oh," said Chris, "one other thing the Governor asked me to ask you."

Confused and not understanding, Natalie responded, "What?"

"The Governor asked if you would like to have a job when you get done playing with airplanes," Chris replied with a smile speeding through the phone lines.

Natalie chuckled looking at the phone. "See you at 9, Condor Terminal, Newark Airport," she replied, and hung up.

Standing up, her back stretching to the ceiling, and a happy smile gracing her now relieved face, she turned toward the office door and yelled, "Margaret, I'm back. What's you got for me?"

Chapter Four

Eight hours is eight hours. It does not matter if it's measured on an expensive watch, an astronomical clock in Strasbourg, a glockenspiel in downtown Munich or a giant sundial in Cave Creek, Arizona. Eight hours is eight hours.

Unless you're sitting in a cigar-shaped cylinder flying 35,000 feet above the earth and traveling at 500 miles per hours. Then, eight hours seems like an eternity.

Relieved only by the waft of fresh air as the door to the plane is opened and the world is let in. Only then does the time sink in. And the clock begins anew.

A large black van pulled up to the bottom of the stairs and a single man got out of the passenger seat and waited at the ground below. He was an elderly gentleman, dressed in a light gray suit, a similar gray hat atop his receding hair-line, hands clasp. His eyes were clear and lucid, his face immobile, and his posture impeccable. He waited as the passengers descended the stairs.

"Herr Zink," said John, "good to see you," as he extended his hand.

The elderly gentleman, a slight smile on his face, grasped the offered hand, bowed slightly and said, "Thank you, good to see you again."

"And kind sir, this is Miss Matthews, Natalie Matthews, CEO of Condor Airlines, our boss."

"Nice to meet you in person, Miss Matthews. We talked several times, but person to person is always better. I had hoped the circumstances would be more pleasant, but in any event, welcome to Germany."

"Herr Zink, nice to meet you also and I must warn you, my name is Natalie. I go by that at home and especially in the office. I would appreciate it if you would refer to me as Natalie. Miss Matthews is someone with whom I am not familiar," she said with a smile.

"Very well, Natalie it shall be. In return, my name is Dieter, Dieter

Zink. Herr Zink was my father. Please call me Dieter."

"All right, all right, enough of the pleasantries," said John with a grin. "These other two gentlemen with us hope to help us with the situation." Pointing to Stick. "This is my father and he prefers to be called Stick. Why is a long story, but I am sure that after a couple of Jägermeisters, it will come out. And this gentleman is Chris Palermo. He is a personal representative of the Governor of the state of New Jersey, home base to Condor Airlines, and accompanies us to provide whatever assistance he and the state can provide. He also is a friend of all of us, and a real smart chap. A different set of eyes to provide a different perspective."

"Thank you all for coming, though the circumstances are less than perfect," said Dieter. "Before entering the van, if you would take a look down the loading dock, you can see the issue for yourself. The plane you see is the one being held hostage. German police, Polizei, keep watch but keep all unnecessary personnel away due to the possibility of a bomb exploding, as the terrorists have threatened. It is unattended other than the maintenance personnel working on the engine and the periodic delivery of food stuffs and drinks, mostly water and soda. We have been granted extra time by the terrorists to fix the engine but that time supposedly runs out in the morning. We have our work to do before then.

"Now, please make yourself comfortable in the van. The trip is short, about ten minutes to my office. We'll set up shop there and work the problem."

While the others gingerly climbed into the van, Stick stood alongside the van and glared at the captured plane, taking in all the possible details of the aircraft, while being hindered by its distance.

He surveyed as one would a doctor prepping a wound, making mental notes concentrating on the physical structure of the plane and storing them for future use. One particular factor he refused to set to memory, instead writing it down on the back of an envelope. That factor, CO-141B, the tail number of the aircraft. Satisfied, he climbed into the van which began its slow but quick journey. He began thinking about the information he carried in his suitcase.

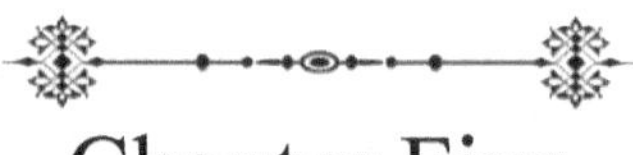

Chapter Five

Herr Zink's office was small compared to the largeness of senior executives in the US, but it was functional, a rather normal desk, couple of not-so-comfortable chairs, a long, flat table behind the desk, and a drab, gray, metal filing cabinet to one side. There was no large table with which to hold discussions with multiple people, but rather a door capable of sliding into the wall, leading to a conference room that could accommodate a large number of people seated around both sides.

Dieter led the way into the conference room, motioning for Natalie to sit at the head of the table, while he sat to her right. The others took seats randomly, without regard to position or grade. A couple of local employees, namely the head of security for the Frankfurt operation and the maintenance director sat down as well.

"Welcome all, though not as pleasant as I had hoped," said Dieter. "Let's start the discussion with an update on the situation from a security perspective. Johann, please give us the latest."

Johann Weiler, head of security for Frankfurt, stood up and addressed the gathering. "Not much has changed since the last update. Three terrorists still hold the plane and its crew as hostage. If they don't leave here soon, they threatened to blow up the plane and kill not only themselves, but the crew as well. We have managed to convince them that an engine has been damaged and needs to be repaired before the plane can fly again, and reluctantly they have extended their demand till tomorrow morning. German police have surrounded the plane, more to keep others away rather than keeping the terrorists blocked in, and are just waiting for instructions. All the options we have discussed seem to end with the loss of life, something we don't want to happen. As of now, we are open to any option that can resolve the situation with a better result."

"Klaus," said Dieter. "What about the maintenance situation?"

Before he could begin, Herr Zink's secretary quietly entered the room and handed him a single piece of paper. He quickly read it and passed it to Natalie.

"Sorry, Klaus, please begin."

"The maintenance is pretty much a farce. We made that up to stall the departure. We chipped a couple of the fan blades, but they are easily replaced in two or three hours. However, we are holding out the possibility of having to replace the whole engine to give us more time to resolve the issue. At least that gives us until tomorrow morning."

"Thank you, Klaus, if anything changes, or if you can think of any more stalling tactics, please let us know. We may need more time."

"Before we go any further, my secretary just handed me a note from the US Embassy, routed through the Consulate here in Frankfurt, that they are sending somebody over who may be able to help us. Don't know who it is or what their position or expertise is, but I welcome any assistance we can get from anyone. We'll continue our discussions and see what they have to offer when they get here."

Natalie nodded in agreement and said, "Anyone have anything to say? Or offer any thoughts?"

Johann, head of security, chimed in, "We have our own security procedures here in Frankfurt, but do not know what your procedures are in the United States. Since this flight originated in the States, is there anything we should know? For instance, are there any weapons or firearms onboard the plane?"

Without hesitation Natalie spoke up. "No, we do not arm our pilots or crew with weapons of any kind. We expect them to safely fly airplanes, not fight a war."

Johann nodded in understanding.

With a slight hesitation, John raised his head and spoke quietly. "That is not entirely correct."

A cone of silence suddenly came over the room. Natalie starred at him, not believing what she heard, the others wondering what he was talking about. Nobody had heard of anything to the contrary.

"Continue, John." The words sliced through the thick silence in the room, each syllable sharpened to a razor's edge.

"Well," said John. "One of the recommendations of the last security audit we conducted concerned the carrying of weapons by the crew. We implemented several of the recommendations, including the secret radio transmitter under the pilot's seat. The recommendation concerning weapons was postponed for further discussion."

"Numerous discussions took place with comments both for and against the proposal being presented. In the end, the conversations ended with the role of the captain of the plane. Like the captain of a ship or vessel, the captain is the law when it comes to his ship. In this case, the ship is an airplane, but the law is the same. The captain is the law. It was then decided that the captain, or in this case, the pilot, should decide if they wanted a weapon or not. It would be up to the pilot. At the final step in operations, before boarding the plane, the pilot would decide and sign a document stating their decision. At that point in time, the weapon would be added to the pilot's flight bag or not. No one, not even the crew, would know if there was a weapon on board. At the end of the flight, the weapon would be returned to the operations personnel. That is where we are today. Captain McHenry chose to have a weapon and it is on the airplane to use as she deems necessary."

The sounds of chairs shifting echoed throughout the room. Natalie looked stunned, shaking her head wondering why she did not know this, but knowing better than to bring that matter up at this moment. A later discussion between her and John was a better choice.

"Well, that is somewhat of a surprise. I would assume that Captain McHenry, being an Air Force officer, has had training in weapons control, along with whatever training we provided, but it sure adds another dimension to our discussion. As much as we may not like it, it must be factored into any solution."

A knock sounded on the conference door leading from the secretary's desk and lobby. "Come in," said Dieter.

The door opened, and a tall, young man, dressed in camouflaged fatigues, with a green beret covering his short hair and a web belt around his waist holding a filled holster, stepped quickly into the conference room, closing the door silently behind him.

He surveyed around the room and noted Natalie at the head of the table. He moved to her side, stopped, and stood at attention.

"Good morning, Ma'am. I am Lieutenant Stephen Bradley, US Army, Special Forces. The US Embassy sent me and my men to see if we can assist in any way. We are here to help."

Chapter Six

A cone of silence immediately descended upon the conference room. While most of the thinking concerning the safety of the crew and airplane had centered around negotiations and prisoner swapping or other non-violent activities, the revelation of a friendly firearm on the plane opened the window for other alternatives, including the possibility of quasi-military action. Add to that the arrival of Lieutenant Bradley and his men, that possibility, and probability, became even stronger.

"Lieutenant," said Natalie, "you said you had other men with you. Could you elaborate on that?"

"Yes, Ma'am, eh, Natalie," stammered the Lieutenant. "I have an additional six men with me, all special forces trained, all with some combat experience from other situations. In addition, two of the six men are accompanied by their canine partners, their dogs. The dogs are trained in detecting explosives. Since a bomb was mentioned in earlier reports, it was thought that their presence would be helpful. In addition, we seem to have all the equipment we need, based on the situation as we see it. Other equipment can be requested, but that will take time, and it seems like time is something we do not have."

"So, Lieutenant, you have the answer," said Natalie.

"No, I don't, Natalie. I don't have THE answer. I have an answer. My experience has shown me that it is not the best answer. People are going to get hurt, maybe die. Things are going to be destroyed, important, but not as important as the people involved. My people and I offer a solution, one of possibly many, but surely not the best solution. Different sides discussing options, negotiating, offering, rejecting, re-offering, rejecting again, and re-offering again until final acceptance, that is the best solution. But if that is not achievable, we are here."

Natalie shook her head in understanding. Violence was not part of her vision of Condor. It never was, and the possibility of it becoming part of its history was disturbing. She held out hope for constructive negotiations and resolutions, but as time went by and options were discussed and discarded, the hope dimmed. And dimmed.

"John, tell me about the weapon that Captain McHenry, Pat, has aboard the aircraft, and how it got there."

John looked around the room at the other occupants, deciding if they had a need to know the security procedure. Only Klaus, the maintenance director, was questionable and John asked him to leave since the information had no relevance to his work or position. Without hesitation, and perhaps with a look of relief, Klaus agreed with the request and left the room. As the door closed, all eyes turned toward John in anticipation of his explanation.

John leaned forward and began. "We talked earlier about how the captain or pilot of the aircraft received the weapon from operations and carried it on the plane. The question, I believe, is how did it get on the plane without being noticed or stopped. As far as being stopped, we negotiated with federal authorities to allow the pilot passage through security screenings with proper authorization, that being a signed declaration from the local Condor security official of the intent to carry a weapon. A verification number was included in case the screening officials questioned the declaration. That has erased that problem, not entirely, but mostly, as some eager screening officials want more assurances from a face-to-face meeting. It rarely happens, but on occasion does.

"As for concealing the weapon, various options were tested with most rejected for multiple reasons, including seeing the pilot wearing a holster and pistol. That panicked a few passengers. It appeared that concealment was the only answer.

"Most of us have seen pilots just prior to boarding an aircraft and most of the pilots are carrying an odd-looking briefcase. Odd because is much larger than the normal business briefcase, hardened all the way around with a stiff card-board substance, and secured with a double flap on the top with a handle from the bottom flap sticking through a slot in the top flap. The case itself is about 20 inches long and about 7 or 8 inches wide. It is not designed for beauty but rather functionality. The inside is divided in two lengthwise by a similar substance. We have all seen them, and they are ugly, but considered a part of the normal crew equipment. Once on-board, the case is placed to the left of the pilot's seat on the cockpit floor between the seat and the fuselage. That is what makes them useful for our purposes.

"Inside the case, on one side of the partition, are two books labeled 'Airport Detailed Information' and further identified as volume one and volume two. They are identical in nature and to the casual observer, are totally harmless. But they are not.

"At least not one. Volume two is completely different. First, it is not a book as the inside is completely hollow. Second, the spine of the book is hinged, allowing it to be opened with a flick of the thumb revealing its contents. It is in here that the weapon is carried, along with a spare clip. After months of testing with current crew members, not professional shooters, this method was chosen. It allows the pilot, most of whom are right-handed to reach across their body as though adjusting a seat strap, open the case, flip open the spine of the fake book with his thumb and reach the other fingers around the weapon, pulling it out of the hollow. In practice, it takes about three seconds from reach to extraction to usage. I say, in practice, because it has never been used. But it is there, all pilots and co-pilots are trained in its use, and available should it be necessary. God forbid it ever is."

Silence filled the room with only a nervous cough breaking the spell.

Chapter Seven

The rest of the day went by quickly. Discussions ensured, options considered, suggestions made and discarded. And frustrations grew. There did not seem to be an answer.

Several conversations with the kidnappers proved fruitless. They were convinced that their act of kidnapping an entire plane with its female crew would make them national heroes when they returned home. They would point out that the Westerners did not have the manhood to fly their own planes and had to rely on females, woman, to do the work.

They would point out how easy it was to kidnap a plane, and its cargo, and just fly it to wherever they wanted. The infidels did not have the courage to defend itself or its property, and thus was ripe for the picking. If they could do it, so could anyone else, and so, go do it!

The frustrations of the Condor group grew as each hour passed along. By mid-afternoon, there was almost complete silence in the conference room as all had run out of ideas for a peaceful resolution to the situation.

Lieutenant Bradley sat quietly at the end of the table, his team having been dismissed to a hotel to rest from the previous exercise and perhaps a future one. If his team were to contribute, it had to start planning now. There was no more time to waste.

"I think we need to move on," said the Lieutenant. "You have given due consideration to all available actions and options but one, and that one is why I am here. We need to start planning for a rescue operation for the crew before it is too late. Agree?"

The group seated around the conference table looked at each other, and looked, and looked, nobody willing to be the first to concede as that being the necessary course of action. Finally, a quiet voice at the end of the table spoke up. It belonged to Stick.

"Look, I don't like bloodshed. The last thing in my mind is to get anybody hurt. But sometimes we don't have a choice. The consequences of not doing anything are too great. I have been in circumstances like this before and didn't like it then and don't like it now."

"Excuse me, Dieter. Nothing personal," Stick inserted as he continued to speak.

"I say we let the Lieutenant and his team do what they are trained to do and that is to get our crew back. The plane and cargo, if lost, is lost, but human lives are saved. And we should be thankful if we can get it done."

And with that, Stick sat back in his seat and waited.

A sigh of relief escaped from the group as though a jail cell door had been opened and freedom regained. Imprisoned by indecisiveness, a way forward had been presented by an old man whose wisdom and plain logical thinking had broken the lock. He waited.

The group continued to look around, judging what other people were thinking. Eventually their gaze turned to the head of the table, to Natalie, CEO of Condor. While their advice was welcomed, it was her who would make the call.

"Lieutenant," she said addressing the camouflaged savior in the room, "how do you plan on rescuing our crew?"

The call had been made.

Chapter Eight

The lieutenant slowly got up from his chair and moved to the end of the table. He softly began to speak, "We knew from the time we got here what our job was going to be if we were called upon to do it. We had no role in the negotiations or the discussions with the terrorists and should not have. That is not our role, not our mission, not why we were sent here. Our role was, and is, to rescue the crew being held hostage. Without all the finery of political repercussions, of international condemnation, of lost equipment or cargo, or any other incidental conditions, our role is to rescue the crew. That is our mission, and while all the discussions have taken place, that is what we have been planning to do. Rest assured that we are not now just starting to plan, nor is this the first rescue we have attempted. There have been others that, for security reasons, we cannot reveal but this is not our first rodeo as we say out west. Let's go over a few things.

"First, the terrorists do not want to hurt or kill the crew. They need the crew to fly them to wherever they desire to go. And they want to show the western man as worthless by letting women fly the aircraft. So, they need to protect the crew.

"Second, they need the plane. How else can they get home? They need the plane to fly them there. If not, they would just blow it up. Why do you think they are waiting for it to get fixed? Because they need it to get home and continue the humiliation of the west, that is why. No, they will not harm the plane.

"Third, they do not care about the cargo. They have rejected without hesitation the trading of the cargo for the crew. They don't want the cargo, they don't care about the cargo, they do not even know what is contained in the cargo. So, any discussions which include the cargo is a non-starter.

"So, what do they care about? They care only about getting home safely and the humiliation of the west. And being true terrorists, with a cause as their backing, the humiliation of the west is more important. If they should die in attempting that, they, in their minds, will still be national heroes.

"We also know that there are three of them, with one of them being the leader who positions himself near the cockpit. And, according to the pilot, stays there pretty much all the time, with an occasional visit to the other two men to check on them. The other two men are positioned on either side of the plane, separated by the cargo load, with the job of watching through the windows for any suspicious activity and repelling or reporting it.

"We also know they have weapons, most likely automatic weapons, as single-shot guns are ineffective. They stay there most of the time, other than to get a little exercise or use the toilet. They are bored and occasionally, napping. They are not professional soldiers but rather 'true believers' on an adventure.

"We have also been led to believe they have a bomb with which to blow up the plane and kill themselves and the crew. While we do not have any proof of that, we have their say so. As such, we have to believe what they say, though we have heard that before without it being true. In any event, we have to act as though it is true.

"So, what do we do? Well, the first item of business is to get inside the plane. There is little we can do from the outside. The question becomes 'How do we get inside the plane?' Previous missions have shown us a couple of ways. One is through the landing gear as there is usually access to the plane through the landing gear bay. However, this requires entering through the fuselage floor, which is a lengthy and noisy process, usually resulting in injury or death to the intruder. A second way is through the pilot's or co-pilot's window. Again, this requires a lift of some sort, crawling headfirst through the window and exposing oneself to sure death. A third method would be to ram the side of the plane with a vehicle large enough to create a hole through which my team can exploit and take down the terrorists before they can do any more damage. This is risky, and quite honestly, not worth it. Once inside, we can handle the business at hand. But that is where we are at the moment. How do we get inside?"

At that moment, Stick stood up at the end of the table.

"I believe I can help you with that problem."

Chapter Nine

All eyes turned toward Stick as the Lieutenant's gaze morphed into a spear, a spear aimed at someone questioning his comments. He and his team had done considerable work up to this point and knew they were right on all fronts.

"Stick, we appreciate your help, but not sure there is anything you can add. How do you think, what do you think, we have missed on our analysis?"

"Lieutenant, I am sure you have a thorough job in researching the various ways to get into the plane. But you missed something, something not too many people know about."

"I assure you, Stick, that we have dissected numerous official Air Force blueprints, drawings, and other documents relating to the C-141. I don't think we missed anything. Can you explain and educate us as to what we missed?"

"Lieutenant, as I said, I am sure you have investigated all approaches to the problem using all available Air Force publications and documents. And I agree, using those documents, there is no other answer you could come up with. But, Sir, these are not now Air Force planes. They are commercial cargo carriers and as such, are not totally representative by the military documents you reviewed. They have changed."

The mood at the conference table shifted a little. A dark cloud had been partially cleared away and a little light began shining through.

"Can you explain, Stick?" the Lieutenant's voice easing in its sharpness.

"Sure, but this may take a minute or two. Please give me the time to explain."

Stick started. "At the end of WW II, the United States had millions of men and tons of equipment all over Europe, a lot of it located in France, which was basically the 'depot' for replacement equipment and ammunition for the front-line troops. When peace came through the defeat of Germany, many senior officials considered the Soviet Union the next most dangerous country in the world. They had considerable equipment and troops and had halted the Germans at Stalingrad, turned the tide, and rushed all the way to Berlin, taking countries, which were supposed to be liberated, under the Soviet government with Soviet sanctioned leaders sympathetic to the communist cause. The concern among the western world was that the Soviets would continue to push westward, all the way to the English Channel and claim all the countries it overran as now part of the Soviet Union, and dared anyone to stop them.

"The western response was to keep the men and equipment in Europe by building military bases in both Germany and France, keeping a force in place designed to keep the Soviets at bay. This worked well until France, under DeGaulle's illusionment that France had won the war and the rest of the free world was not necessary, decided to evict all foreign elements from France. In the case of the United States, the closing of military bases in France and the moving of troops out of the country was called FRELOC, or France Relocation. And now the interesting part.

"The cost of maintaining all the troops in Europe was causing problems back here in the States. Besides the monetary cost, the political cost of keeping troops overseas when the war was over and the fighting done, was building. The powers that be decided that the troops and their families should return home but the equipment would stay in Germany, in specially built controlled-humidity warehouses where they could be maintained, but be available if needed. The only thing required to reactivate the fighting force was to add the men, while the remaining divisions in Germany would act as a restraining force, not meant to defeat a Soviet attack but rather to slow them down and provide time to reintroduce the men to their stored equipment and move into position. To do that would require a large force of transports capable of carrying hundreds of troops across the ocean. Thus, was born the C-141 with its unique capability of meeting that requirement. Over two hundred were manufactured and stationed around the country and Reforger (Return of Forces to Germany) exercises were instituted to demonstrate the return capability, both to our allies, but also to the Soviets.

"But a problem arose due to the passage of time.

"The equipment in the storage facilities became obsolete. Technology had passed them by and the tanks and artillery pieces were no longer, along with other equipment, suitable for a modern war. They had to be replaced, and were replaced over the years with new, more modern equipment, which in turn revised the concept of just ferrying men to Europe, but now having men AND equipment sent to Europe. And that equipment, both in terms of size and weight, out-grew the capacity of the C-141, especially the weight requirements. Larger, more capable planes were built making the C141's less in demand, and resulted in many of them being grounded while still requiring the cost of maintenance and overhaul.

"To solve that problem while still maintaining an active fleet, the Air Force sold excess C-141's. Repeating the strategy of the tug boats in New York harbor after WWII, the planes were sold at rock bottom prices with the provision that they be maintained in flying condition for a minimum of five years. Your father, Natalie, bought four of those planes for his fledging business and had them modified, with Air Force concurrence, to be more suitable for commercial use.

"And so, Lieutenant, that is why a review of existing Air Force drawings and diagrams did not reveal a new door. In their mind, it did not exist."

Natalie, intrigued by the discussion, asked what modifications were made to the planes.

Stick replied, "The biggest modification was the making of cargo doors on the side of the fuselage, allowing forklifts to load from the side. It resulted in faster loading and unloading times with larger pallet loads compared to the rear ramp of the C-141. This made the rear ramp unnecessary except in unusual cases, and in the commercial application, was hardly used at all. However, crew members still wanted to be able to enter the fuselage from the rear of the aircraft and not have to walk to the front of the plane and board through the cabin door.

"So, a rear entry door was added to the ramp which could be opened when necessary and which allowed access to the interior without lowering the ramp. That, Lieutenant, is how I believe your team can get inside the plane."

"Stick, I know you have been around for a while, but how do you know this," asked the Lieutenant.

"Lieutenant," came the response. "Let me explain something to you which has haunted me for some time."

"What you see before you is an old man. There is no doubt about that. But that has not always been the case. In fact, I was born at a very young age and worked very hard to get old. Some of it was fun, some not so much fun. But it all happened. Along the way, I experienced a lot of things. Following 35 years in the Army, I worked in the airplane industry, some large corporations, some small repair shops in rural America. But always airplanes. One of my stops was Lockheed, the manufacturer of the C-141 and the contractor used for the commercialization of the same airplane. In fact, I worked on the commercialization. In fact, I worked on the ramp of the same airplane. In fact, Lieutenant, after checking with buddies working in the Pentagon aircraft records department, I installed the ramp-door on the plane that is sitting on the tarmac.

"That, Lieutenant, is how I know."

With the realization to whom he was speaking, the Lieutenant stood up a little straighter and said, "Mr. Stick, would you join my team and I in the adjoining room so we can discuss tonight's operation?"

Chapter Ten

The sun had sunken below the horizon and millions of lights lit up the entire airport. One lone C-141 sat at the end of the loading terminal, tail number CO-141B, under the glare of portable spotlights placed around the whole plane as if to show it off to the world.

Behind the plane and all the others waiting for permission to fly was a well-used service road, navigated by vehicles bringing catering items, fuel, cleaning supplies, and anything else needed by the planes and their crews.

Occasionally, a black van would cross behind all the planes, following other vehicles in turn and proceed to its destination. In ten to twenty minutes, the same van would again traverse the same route, in the opposite direction, only to return in another ten to twenty minutes. It blended into the flow of service vehicles so as not to cause alarm to anyone observing the scene. About an hour into the exercise, the black van on its usual route, moved to the side of the service road, shut down its lights, relying on reflectors from being hit, and waited.

As if on command, the portable spot lights illuminating the plane blinked, dimmed, then shut off completely. This was not unexpected as the terrorists had demanded the lights be turned off at night to facilitate their observation of the tarmac surrounding the plane while lessening the ability of outside observers to see the happenings and movements inside. It also enabled the rescue team to move unseen to its assigned positions.

A couple of minute later, a squawk came on the hidden receiver in the cockpit and spoke quietly. "Captain McHenry, the time has come. Please have your briefcase ready in case it is needed. Listen for the click." The receiver went silent in the cockpit.

"Lieutenant, our observation post observes no unusual activity. You are cleared to move into position and begin the operation."

Without turning on its lights, the black van made a left turn and proceeded to the airplane, stopping directly behind the fuselage and just short of the loading ramp. To the plane's occupants, it was invisible. Quickly, eight men and two dogs jumped from the side door of the van and moved to the ramp. They all crouched down and remained silent.

A minute later, the Lieutenant gave the signal and two agile men, and one not so agile, moved to the ramp. Stick ran his hand over the ramp door until it found the hidden access to the ramp door. He pulled a strange metal object from his pocket. It was shaped like a hex wrench with a 90-degree bend at one end and a small but thick extrusion from the bent portion of the tool. Finding the door's lock access, he inserted the small tool into the recess, jostled it around to ensure contact, then turned to the Lieutenant and nodded.

The Lieutenant acknowledged the signal and motioned for the remaining soldiers and dogs to follow him. They deliberately and quietly moved beneath the fuselage till they were under the main door and a couple of feet from the roll-away stairs. The soldiers crouched and waited, the dogs lying quietly, their muzzles preventing them from barking. The Lieutenant double clicked his microphone, and Stick went into action.

The extrusion on the strange tool pushed down on the access lock and allowed the hex tool to activate the locking device. Slowly the ramp door released itself from its sealed recluse and began lowering itself into a loading position, similar to the position stairs on a private jet would assume. The hydraulics of the door allowed it to lower smoothly and quietly until the top of the door reached the ground and it settled itself. Stick moved away from the door and motioned for the two soldiers to enter.

Quietly and carefully the two soldiers, using their night vision goggles, climbed the stairs and found themselves at the point of the aircraft where the ramp joined the main fuselage. A large canvas curtain hanging from the top of the fuselage to the deck provided visual security but with the thrust of a sharp knife and a careful cut of a doorway, easily allowed the two soldiers entry into the main cargo deck.

Giving each other a thumbs up, they moved into their respective positions, one on the port side looking up toward the cock-pit and the other on the starboard side, looking in the same direction. They knelt, peering round the cargo, their night goggles transforming the darkness inside the plane into a green-tinted scene clearly showing portions of the two terrorists resting against the cargo and peering out the plane's windows.

All the soldiers needed now was for the terrorists to move and reveal more of their bodies to ensure a quick hit and rapid demise. None was forthcoming.

The sergeant on the port side slowly withdrew his knife from its scabbard. He rapped it a couple of times on the fuselage wall and then threw it down the walkway, the knife clanking as it careened between the wall and the cargo. The sudden noise startled the dozing guard and he turned to see what caused it.

There are small and subtle differences between a professional soldier and a pretender. The differences can mean living or dying. In this case, it meant dying.

The terrorist spun around to investigate the noise made by the thrown knife and as he did so, the left side of his flak jacket flew open, the same side a professional soldier would have zipped up to protect his chest. The red dot of the laser aiming device, bore-sighted to the line of the rifle barrel, clearly illuminated the target. A split second later, the "Wop" of a single bullet smashed into the chest of the terrorist and staggered him backwards. He looked down to see blood soaking his shirt, just in time to hear a second "Wop," and a second bullet tearing his heart apart.

With a glazed look in his eyes, he fell to his knees, then, as though in slow motion, leaned forward till he lay spread-eagled on the deck. His now-useless rifle clanged against the metal wall.

The second terrorist on the other side of the plane heard the noise and rose to look at what the fuss was all about. That was all it took. With the squeeze of a single finger, the hurtling bullet found its target, knocking it down and ending its being.

Only the head terrorist remained. And he was determined to find the noise and quiet it. Pointing his rifle down the length of the cargo hold, he took one step in that direction while turning his attention to where his men were located. Seeing neither, he took another step, now standing completely outside the cockpit area.

Captain McHenry saw the opportunity and didn't hesitate to take it. With one smooth motion, she swung her right arm across her chest to the waiting briefcase. Her thumb quickly opened the fake book spine, her fingers sliding into the hollow book, retrieving the weapon inside.

Glancing quickly at the distracted terrorist, she swung her gun-carrying arm back across her chest and toward the assailant's head. Sensing her movement, the terrorist raised his shoulder deflecting the gun's barrel from hitting him squarely in the head, but still suffering a staggering blow causing him to take a couple of weak steps.

He glanced over at her with daggers shooting from his eyes and turned to aim his rifle at her. Before he could, she swung her arm again, the pistol's barrel landing just above his ear, sending him sprawling to the deck, unconscious. Pat moved to straddle the prone body, aiming the gun at his head as though daring him to move.

In a voice which left no doubt, she instructed the co-pilot to clear the rifle and throw it out her window to the tarmac below and ordered the navigator to turn on the cabin lights and open the crew door, letting in whoever might be there.

The crew responded without hesitation.

As soon as Lieutenant Bradley heard the crew door latch begin to move, he ordered the two remaining soldiers to grab the stairs and move them to the plane and the opening door. He leapt over the stair railing and ran up the moving stairs, arriving at the door just as the navigator was sliding it out of the way.

With a solid push, he moved the door aside, motioned her out of the way, and rushed to the pilot standing guard over the motionless terrorist. With a calmness honed by previous actions, he stepped in front of the pilot, knelt down and checked for a pulse on the neck of the man, finding a faint one.

Grabbing the terrorist's hands, he wrapped them around his back and using military ties, secured them together, rendering them useless should he awake.

Standing erect, the Lieutenant looked at the shaken pilot and said, "Ma'am, could you put the pistol on the table. We don't want any accidents at this point."

The frozen pilot began to thaw, understanding that the nightmare was over. She cautiously placed the pistol on the navigator's table and stepped back. With a sigh of relief, she sat down on the center instrument console, covered her eyes with trembling hands, and let the waters of stress stream down her face.

The Lieutenant motioned for the dog handlers to begin their bomb search with the hope of finding nothing. Fifteen minutes later that hope was realized and the clean-up, both physically and emotionally, began.

Chapter Eleven

Whew!

An uncontrollable collective sigh of relief filled the conference room as the last of the interrogators closed the door behind them. It seemed like a great weight had been lifted from their shoulders and they were now free to move as they pleased.

The soldiers had left first, after a filling breakfast, and the plane crew followed shortly thereafter, returning to the hotel to continue catching up on lost sleep. The final interviewers, members of the German National Security Administration, stayed another half an hour or so before wrapping up their questions, oh so many questions, and leaving.

The four Americans and one German were now left alone, a status they had hoped would come sooner, but glad that, in fact, it had arrived at all. Several stood up to stretch their legs and grab a lingering Danish. A few rested their heads on their arms stretched out on the table. But they all relished the fact that it was over. They now could go on with their respective duties, chores, and lives. Behind them lay an amazing episode in their lives and before them, well who knew.

Dieter placed his hands on the table, palms down, and pushed himself into an upright position. "Natalie," he said, "what are your plans now?"

Before she could speak, Stick interjected, "Could we visit the crash site? I would like to pay my respects to Jack, my co-pilot, who died there. Can we do that?"

"You mean the plane that crashed during the Berlin Blockade on the return trip from Berlin? I believe your father, Natalie, was the pilot of that plane and was saved by one of the crew-members. Is that right?"

"Yes," said Natalie, looking at Stick. "And Jack, Jack Scofield, was the co-pilot. He didn't make it out."

"Of course, we can do that if there are no objections," said Dieter, looking at Natalie. She nodded in the affirmative.

"How about you, Natalie, are you going right home?"

Natalie hesitated for a moment, then responded. "You know, Dieter, I have never been to Germany before. Perhaps I will take a little time a see some things. Germany is a relatively small country and if you can loan me one of the company's cars, I may stay around for a couple of days. For sure I would like to visit Oberstdorf, which is where my father stayed until the accident and his evacuation to Walter Reed Hospital. He told me how beautiful the country was, especially the southern part, and I would like to experience it. Can that be arranged? I can drive myself if a car is available."

"A car is not a problem. I will have one of my people take you to the crash site. When done, you can drop him off here and drive to Oberstdorf. It is not far and the road is well marked. You and whoever wants to stay, can remain at the hotel until departure, whenever that is. Does that work?"

Natalie nodded and Dieter excused himself to go to his office and make the arrangements. A few minutes he came back with a young man he introduced as Jurgen. "He'll take you to the crash site," Dieter said.

They all rose and headed to the waiting car, Stick leading the pack like a shepherd leading his flock.

He was going back.

Chapter Twelve

The black Mercedes pulled up alongside the grass now lining the abandoned runway and crawled to a stop. To anyone standing outside the car, it looked like a one-vehicle funeral procession. To those inside, it was. Stick opened the passenger's front door and gingerly stepped onto the cracked concrete, now weathered by nature and time.

He looked around the area as though recreating that day as the others exited from the back seat and stood still waiting for him to move. Eventually he slowly moved around the front of the car, his left hand using the car hood to steady his steps, his right hand stuck in his pants pocket.

The square marble stump seemed out of place amid the un-mowed grass, its top barely visible among the growth. Stick moved quietly through the grass, moving his head, and looking for any signs, any indications, any hints at all, of the tragic events that had occurred at that spot years ago. Other than the marble monument, there were none. Other than his memory, there were none.

As Stick approached the marble stone, etched letters began to emerge. "Jack Scofield" formed the top row and just below the name, the day, month and year, "19 October 1948" appeared. He remembered that day as though it was yesterday. And someplace in his mind, it was.

Stick reached the stone and, like an old man, knelt down on his right knee and bowed. His eyes filled with tears as he remembered his crewmate, the times they had together and, more importantly, the last time he saw him. Behind him, but not to close, stood his three companions, like a white picket fence enclosing a precious spot, forbidding others to enter while a service was on going. They stood quietly and watched, trying to fathom the unrelenting thoughts going through the penitent's mind, without a clue to help.

"Jack," murmured Stick through lips closed in pain, "I am sorry I left you. I checked, I honestly did, and you had no signs of still being with us. There was no pulse, there was no breathing, there was no movement, there was nothing. Your eyes, though open, were glazed open and stared straight ahead. Your head was tilted at a strange angle. I thought you were gone." Sobs interrupted the laments, his head being held by his left hand now perched on a bent left leg, his right leg quivering but still anchored to the ground. His chest heaved as though breathing for two.

"I moved to Ron and discovered he was still alive. Automatically I began cutting loose his harnesses and trying to free him from his seat. Meanwhile, the flames outside the plane were moving closer to the main fuel tanks and the blast which would surely follow. I had no choice, Jack. I had to get him out. Finally cutting through the straps, I pulled him from his seat, loaded him on my back and started to the rear of the torn fuselage.

"Before taking the first step, I looked back at you in your seat. In a moment that will be forever imbedded in my mind, I saw your arm move. I screamed for you, Jack. I screamed as loud as I could. You didn't answer. I was confused. I was frozen in place. My mind was racing in all different directions. How could I leave you there to die? How could I carry both you and Ron out at the same time? I had read about people doing super-human things when it was needed and I thought I could get you both out of the plane.

"I turned and started back to you as your arm moved again. I couldn't tell if it was an involuntary movement, a movement caused by the plane's condition, or if it was you signaling something. And if it was you, I was not going to leave you there.

"I started back to get you when the flames reached the cockpit window. I knew, then, there was no way to reach you and carry both you and Ron to safety. My training said, 'take what you can' and move on. And that is what I did.

"Jack, I cannot say the word sorry enough, warranted or not. I cannot get it through my mind that your signals, voluntary or not, urged me to take Ron and move on. I cannot forget, I won't forget, I don't want to forget what happened. And I ask for your forgiveness for whatever reason you find acceptable. I'm sorry.

"Jack, one more thing." Stick's right hand emerged for his pants pocket holding a bright shiny object. "The other day I received this medal for saving Ron's life. While I appreciated it, I did what any soldier would have done, facing the same circumstances. But I want you to have it. Because, while I risked my life to save his, you gave your life for the same reason.

"Rest peacefully, my dear friend, till we meet at the Club for a cold one. I love you."

With a couple of digs with his right hand, Stick opened the ground and gingerly placed the Soldier's Medal in the shallow grave. He covered it up with the dirt removed and scattered remnants of pulled grass over the top to hide it.

With his remaining strength, he stood up as straight as an old man could, and saluted. Dropping the salute, he turned around and walked to his friends still standing guard. He continued past them toward the car, his limp slowly returning.

Chris and John turned to follow Stick. Natalie stood still for a minute, said, "I'll be right there," and walked to the marble stone. She knelt where Stick had knelt and slowly rescued the shiny medal for its earthy grave, putting it in her pocket.

"Thank you, Jack, for understanding. Rest easy."

The ride back to the office was eerily quiet.

Chapter Thirteen

The black Mercedes pulled up in front of the Condor operations center door and stopped. Jurgen got out and stood by the car door holding the keys to the ignition like the clapper in a bell.

"Who wants the keys?" he asked, looking around.

At the same instant, two car doors opened. Natalie emerged from the front passenger seat and started around the front of the car to get the keys. Chris extracted himself from the rear seat behind the driver. They both arrived at Jurgen at the same time, each reaching for the keys as though it was their sworn duty to take possession of the prized objects and use them as needed. They both stopped short as they recognized the other's intent.

"I'll drive," said Natalie as she reached for the keys.

"Nah, that's all right, I'll take care of that," said Chris as he too reached for the keys.

"Not to worry, I got this," she said.

"Nope. It's my job, that's what I came along for."

"Look," said Natalie. "This is a company car, a Condor car. And I am the CEO of Condor. So, it's my car, and I'll drive, period."

"No," retaliated Chris. "I was asked to come along to provide support, practically begged to—"

"I did not beg," interrupted Natalie.

"—well, it sounded like begging to me."

The sound of the glaring between the two was unnerving.

"Children. Children. Children. There is no need to quibble over a simple matter," said John as he moved between them. "I'm sure we can figure this out to all's satisfaction. It seems like a simple question of who gets to drive the car. Both of you want to do it, for different reasons. One feels she has the right to do it, and the other feels he has the obligation to do it. Alas, I feel both arguments have merit. However, let's go back to the 'why' we are here and see if that makes a difference."

"Natalie, why are you here?"

"John, I don't think this is necessary."

"Natalie, please just answer the question."

With a sigh, Natalie thought for a minute, then answered. "First, I came to help resolve the situation with the hi-jacking of the plane and the safety of the crew. Second, I was hoping to take the time to learn a little about my mother's country, partake in its culture and perhaps meet some long-lost relatives."

"And Chris, how about you?"

"Well," said Chris, "I was begged, oops excuse me, I was strongly requested to come along to provide, I assume, some measure of moral support. Driving the car would be part of that as it would give Natalie a chance to achieve her second objective, that of learning about her mother's country. It is kind of difficult to do that while driving a hundred miles an hour on the Autobahn with a red Porsche blinking its headlights and sounding its horn behind you wanting to pass. Oh, and not to mention the driver giving you the universal unity sign of one finger pointing upward as he zips by. You're bound to miss a little culture there."

Natalie glared at Chris. He had made his point, but she was not going to concede. She abruptly turned and stomped her way around the car, a scowl on her face but a smile in her heart.

They both got into their seats and Chris started the powerful engine. With a hint of humor Chris said, "What are these letters for by the gear thingy."

Natalie looked at him, not knowing if he was serious or kidding. He looked at her and gave her an "I got you" grin.

The smile got a little bigger as the tires squealed pulling away from the building.

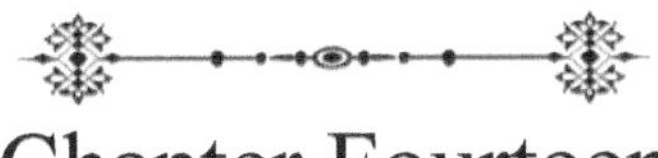

Chapter Fourteen

Chris's anticipation grew as he smoothly drove down the local highway toward the Autobahn. His anxiety almost reached its peak as the blue and white Autobahn sign approached, pointing to the on-ramp on the left. He swung the wheel left and started to pick up speed until the realization hit.

The realization that the area of the Autobahn he had to drive was under construction. Suddenly that thought of driving a hundred miles per hour—legally—was thwarted by the line of huge trucks pulling equally huge trailers chugging on what should have been a raceway. Signs reading 80 KPH eased some of the frustration until he realized that 80 KPH translated into 50 MPH at home.

"Hell," he thought, "some people do that at home in parking lots." With a sigh of resignation, he slowed down and eased into the flow of traffic. Natalie looked over and tried to keep from laughing but her lips just wouldn't listen, and they bent a little at the edges. They settled in for a short, but long, drive.

The exit for Oberstdorf loomed ahead and Chris happily swung the car through the exit and onto the two-lane highway. Two kilometers down the road, a yellow sign announced the presence of the town and, cresting the top of a small hill, Chris pulled the Mercedes onto a dirt area inviting visitors to stop and view the village from its vantage point and, perhaps, to say a little prayer to the little wooden statue atop a pole and surrounded by the façade of a church. These statues were randomly placed along country roads inviting travelers to stop and rest while viewing the vistas surrounding them. They served to relieve the tensions of the road and give the right foot a chance to rest.

Natalie got out of the car and walked to the top of the hill, peering down on the little village that was her beginning. The town spread out before her like a quilt of different scenes. She saw the one main street through the village, she saw the old homes carefully aligned with the street and the swept and well-kept sidewalks and even gutters which fronted the homes. She laughed at the absence of traffic lights and the lack of people on the streets. It was nothing like home. And she loved it!

A tiny tear formed in her eye and she closed the lids to wipe it away. And the transformation began.

The single village street magically morphed into a wooden drawbridge spanning the shimmering moat, flanked on both sides by gatehouses now with ramparts and towers, sporting the flags and banners of the inhabitants. A blue and white hue spread from the bottom of the scene onto the dull houses, slowly turning them into beacons of light leading the way to another world, a world of color, of hope, of cheer, and most of all, of love.

The widening hue bathed every house as it spread throughout the village, erasing the age-old dirt and dust and washing it with the beauty of color. At the center of the village, an old fountain, once the source of water for the village but long ago dried up, suddenly spurted forth its life-giving gift. It's mist, pierced by the rays of the sun, created a cacophony of lights, a light-show in the air, a light-show through which he rode.

He rode aboard a snow-white stead, whose shiny armor made it seemed like it was floating. A long mane waved in the slight wind and the hoofs shone like gem-stones, amazing the on-lookers as he moved gently past them. The knight, adorned with glittering armor, a gem crusted sword hanging from a golden belt, and a white silk scarf streaming from his helmet, scanned the crowd gathered around as if he was seeking someone. Slowly moving, he never missed a face.

As if by magic, the mount stopped and turned slightly to the right. A moment that seemed like an eternity passed, and the knight reached for and removed his helmet, his angelic face now visible for all to see.

"Ingrid, is that you?" questioned the knight of the realm.

"Natalie, it's time to move on. We are getting a little hungry," said Chris.

Natalie slowly turned to Chris. "My mother always told me about a white knight who would visit her and they would spend the rest of their lives together in happiness and love. I was just thinking about that, seeing the village."

"I know," said Chris.

"How do you know," questioned Natalie. "You never met her."

"I know. Merlin is a friend of mine."

The four friends got into the car and crossed the drawbridge.

Chapter Fifteen

The outside door closed just as the inside door opened and the four Americans quickly entered the dining room of the Gasthaus. Any doubt as to their nationality was quickly erased by their loafers and button-down shirts.

The group surveyed the interior like the visitors they were, two of them pilgrims, seeking the Holy Grail of generations gone-by, and visits and long-ago stories relayed to them by previous villagers, and two of them tourists, taking in the traditional trappings of a local eatery and beer pub serving the local population with little or no pretense of splendor or grandeur.

Each had a different perspective; each had a different reason for being there, and each had a specific goal to achieve, some knowing and some not knowing.

Two oval sitting booths were to the right of the door. up against the wall. One was unoccupied, while the second seated an elderly couple, obviously enjoying their visit, and a third, equally elderly woman, apparently a worker at the gasthaus, clothed in a bright apron strong around her neck and tied at the waist, joining in their visit. A silence fell upon them as they watched the newcomers enter the premises, wondering what these Americans were doing in this out-of-the-way place usually visited only by locals of the village. It seemed strange and the hush embellished the feeling.

The aproned woman got up from her seat and approached the four-some. "Darf Ich bitte, Helfen?" she said in her native tongue, asking if she could help them.

While three of the group looked stunned, the fourth, Natalie, responded quickly, "Ya, bitte, wir haben hunger. Konnen wir etwas sum essen haben?"

"Naturlich," said the elderly woman. "Bitte, kommen Sie mit," as she led them to a scattering of tables away from the door.

The Americans followed her to the other end of the dining room where four or five round tables stood. Four of them were of regular size with plenty of room for the party. One table, considerably larger than the others and sporting a wrought iron sign, sat in the midst of them all.

Out of instinct, Chris grabbed a chair from the larger table and started to sit down. Instantly, Stick grabbed his arm and motioned him to not sit there. Chris shot a questioning glance at Stick, wondering what was going on. In response Stick mouthed, "I'll tell you later, just follow the woman."

With a sigh of relief, the elderly woman pointed to one of the other tables and motioned them to seat themselves. As they did, the woman responded, "Ich komme zuruck." Natalie translated for the others and explained that she said she would be right back, probably with menus and asking for drinks.

In a few short minutes, the woman came back with menus and a middle-aged man, and a huge smile on her face. "This is my son," she explained. "He is the owner here and the chef. And he speaks real good English, much better than I. He will help you."

The man bowed a little and said his name was Tomas. "This is my gasthaus," he said. "Here are the menus, the English version on the reverse side to better understand what we serve. Are there any questions?"

The four Americans looked at each other. Finally, John spoke up. "How did you learn to speak English so well, Tomas?"

Tomas laughed. "Thank you for noticing. When I was going to school, it was mandatory to take English, so for several years I studied English there. Upon graduation, and following my cooking career, I worked at several different restaurants, most of which catered to English-speaking clientele. But mostly, I learned English when I was working in England at a restaurant in London. It was there that I learned the most. And of course, with the English penchant for doing it their way, I learned it the English way, and it has stuck, though it has since lost some of its haughtiness." Tomas laughed again.

"So you came back home and opened this gasthaus?" asked John.

Tomas laughed again. "No," he answered. "This gasthaus has been in the family for a long time. You see, here in Germany, it is usual that once a family member obtains something, like a farm, or store, or gasthaus, it usually stays in the family, from generation to generation. That is the case here. When my father passed, the gasthaus was given to me to work and use it to support my family. It was a good idea since I like the business and enjoy the cooking."

"So, your father opened the gasthaus?" asked John.

"Actually, no. His father, my grandfather, opened it. Well, not quite true. It was given to him by my grandfather's brother who had opened it."

"Wow, that was very generous of him," said John.

"Yes, it was. But actually, it was kind of forced on him. See my grandfather's brother was wounded during WWI and lost a leg. Nobody would hire him because of it so in desperation he opened a small imbiss, or food wagon. It became so successful that he was able to buy this location, renovated it, and named it after his wife, Rose. Hence the name 'zum Rose' or 'to Rose.'"

"They did very well, had a little girl they named Ingrid, and were enjoying life until the Nazis came to power and WW II started. During the early stages of the war, it went well for Germany, or the Nazis' and for most people, things were pretty normal. However, after the invasion in France, the war took a nasty turn and it began to rain on Germany. At that time, Kurtz, his formal name was Herr Kurtz but we called him by his last name, Kurtz, he decided to move his family out of Germany, and out of the war, to a small town in France. So, he left, and following the German tradition, gave the gasthaus to my grandfather. So, from there to my father and later to me. And here we are."

"Sorry for so many questions," said John, "but Kurtz never returned to the village?"

"No," said Tomas. "Sadly, Rose, the wife, was killed in a tragic accident in France. A German fighter plane lost a dogfight with an American fighter and crashed into a farmhouse where Rose was making dinner. She never survived and, in fact, was never recovered because the fire consumed the house. That was enough for Kurtz, and he left France with his daughter and emigrated to America. They apparently found a German settlement in the American Midwest and settled there, doing something. Ingrid, the daughter, apparently had a child, we heard a daughter but know very little about her. The last my mother heard was that Kurtz had passed away, Ingrid was living alone, and the daughter had gone to a university on the East coast of America. Since then, there has been nothing."

"Well, actually there was one thing," said the old woman as she pulled a piece of crumpled paper from what looked like an address book out of her apron pocket. "We received this, an obituary from Ingrid's death sent by one of her friends where she lived Besides the details, it mentions a daughter, Natalie Kurtz, from New Jersey. But there is nothing else. We searched later but with no results. She is either gone or changed her name. In any event, we could not locate her."

Tomas' mother neatly folded the obituary and returned it to the address book, patting it softly to make sure it was secure and to tell it that it was still loved.

Silence surrounded the table. The only emotion was Stick's intent stare into the watery eyes of the woman sitting across the table from him.

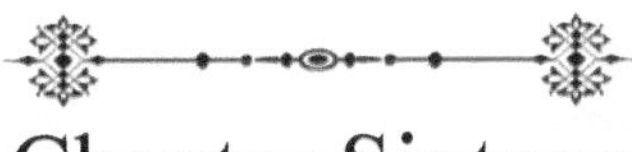

Chapter Sixteen

The silence was deafening. The only sound was the quiet sobbing of the elderly woman whose thoughts now centered on the ones she had lost. She bent over and rested her face on her hands, trying to wipe the tears before they ran down her entire face. Her tired body began to shake, and Tomas grabbed a chair and helped his mother slowly sit down.

Her elbows resting on her knees, her head held aloft by her hands, and the sounds of internal pain slowly emitted from the human. Slowly and quietly, she began to speak, as though talking to herself.

"She was my best friend. We did everything together. We played, we ate, we rode the school bus, we went to the same school. People knew us as two. We were cousins, but in our minds, we were twins. And we were called Twins. Whether it was because our names were so close, she was Ingrid and I was Sigrid, or because we were always together. Where you found one, you found the other. When our families traveled, the other one came along. There was no leaving her behind. Parents knew it. It was useless for them to argue. The Twin came.

"Even when we started different gymnasiums because of different courses of study, we still spent most of the day together talking about girl things, about sports, even about boys. And when we went to different Universities, we still looked for each other after class. We studied together, we went to lectures together, we walked the school parks together. We basically grew up, and up, and up together."

Sigrid raised her head and looked at her raptured audience. There was no sign of boredom, only what was coming next. And she continued.

"When her mother was killed in France, things started to change a little. Her admiration for the German soldier fighting for his country diminished. Her loss had triggered her resentment toward the military, and it turned out, toward anyone who wore a uniform, be it military, polizei, or even postamt workers. Her hatred centered on pilots for her mom's death as it was caused by a fighter plane crashing into the farmhouse where her mom was making dinner for the family. A dinner never served, and a hatred never fully released. While we would talk about it, and about death and how it felt, what happened after, and if there was a loving God, why did he permit men to fight and kill each other, not to mention innocent people who felt no ill-will toward others. Why did that happen? And there was no answer other than the shaking of heads and the daily hug that said it all.

"But that all changed one evening here in the gasthaus. A new American pilot was having dinner when a couple of Nazi youths began attacking her father, an old man with only one real leg, because he was not a Nazi and didn't want to be. It happened right there, against the wall under the steps. The American pilot left his seat and tried to stop the beating. Initially successful, he was soon overwhelmed and sent to the floor with kicks and blows, only to survive when Ingrid called the Polizei for help. The Ploizei originally tried to arrest the pilot until Ingrid intervened and told them what happened. From that moment on, she and the pilot became a thing. Oh, we talked about it and she told me how interesting and wonderful he was and that they were seeing a lot of each other until he was gone, never to show up at the gasthaus again.

"Ingrid was devastated. First her mother had gone, now what could have been a true love had disappeared without a trace. We talked, not as often, but we talked. When her dad moved and took her to France, anticipating another war because of the Soviets' blockade of Berlin, and onward to America, it was over. A few letters and notes now and then. A birth notice about a little girl shortly after she got to America. She named the girl Natalie, and the note said she wanted her to merge into the American culture and thought a German name would be rejected because of the wars. I searched everywhere I could, papers, libraries, university rosters, all to no avail. My friend, my lifelong friend was gone and I couldn't even find her daughter. I have yet to accept it. The world has accepted the loss. I have not.

"I miss her," she sobbed into her hands. "I truly miss her."

Without a word, Natalie slowly pushed her chair back and moved to Sigrid's side. She knelt down and took the aged hands into her own and bowed her head next to Sigrid's.

With a trembling voice, Natalie whispered, "You are not alone. I miss her also, as a daughter misses her mother. For she was my mother and I am her daughter, as you are my cousin. My name is Natalie. Natalie Kurtz Matthews. And I have come home."

Chapter Seventeen

The whisp of chilled air snaked through the two open doors as the young girl entered and turned to hang her coat onto the generations old coat rack which stood by the door as a sentinel would to a castle.

The chatting and laughing at the far table aroused her curiosity and she glanced over to see the source of the noise. At the same time, the unwelcomed air reached the ankles of the elderly woman sitting at the table and she turned to investigate the cause of the chill.

"Sophie," cried out Sigrid. "Bitte komm hier. Komm schnell!"

Sophie smiled and quickly walked over to her grandmother at her request. She bent down and kissed her cheek, then reached up and gave her father a huge hug. With an angelic smile, she faced the remainder of the table and said, "Hello."

The grandmother's wrinkled fingers intertwined with the young girl's smooth skin as she said, "Sophie, do you remember me talking about my best friend, Ingrid, the woman who went to America when she was about your age because her father was afraid another world war was going to start over the Berlin Blockade?"

Sophie smiled and replied, "Yes, of course, she was your best friend. You were always telling me stories about the two of you and your adventures and all the fun you had together, how neither family could go away without the additional tag-a-long, and how she apparently fell in love with an American soldier."

"Yes," said Sigrid, with a smile on her face. "It was a good time till she had to leave with her father. We wrote a few letters but that soon stopped. I was really sad when that happened."

"Yes, I know," said Sophie. "You would always be happy talking about the letters you got. Except the one with her obituary notice."

"I know, that was a sad part of my life. But also, a good part as it identified her daughter, Natalie, whom I knew nothing about. It opened up a whole new door."

"Good for you," said Sophie.

"So, my grandchild, I would like you to meet a dear relative of mine," gesturing toward Natalie. "We just met today, though it was years in the making. Sophie, this is your cousin, Natalie, from the United States. She came to visit."

Sophie was stunned. She looked over at Natalie who had a shy smile on her face while mouthing "hello." After a moment's hesitation, Sophie moved behind her grandmother and walked over to Natalie.

Natalie's smile grew broader as she extended her hand in greeting. Sophie rushed over the last couple of feet between them and brushing aside the extended hand, she wrapped her body around Natalie's and hugged tightly.

Loosening the hug, she looked at Natalie and said, "Shaking hands are for friends and neighbors, not for family. Hugs are for family and you are my family, my long-lost cousin, and I am very happy to meet you as you reconnect your mother with my grandmother. Welcome to the family."

Natalie sat there with moisture welling in her eyes. She, indeed, was home.

Chapter Eighteen

The euphoric feeling came crashing down like a broken window as Natalie exclaimed, "Oh no, I completely forgot! Oh God, I'm sorry!"

"What? What's the matter? What happened? What's going on?" chorused the people around the table.

And with a slightly sheepish grin, she replied, "With all the good times and wonderful thoughts being brought back to life, I completely forgot to introduce my fellow travelers sitting around the table. Forgive me, guys."

"Yes, you did," said Sigrid. "And we apologize, gentlemen, for not asking. So, Natalie, who are these fine gentlemen, especially the young one there, who seems especially taken with our latest arrival."

Natalie smiled and began. "Well, the older gentleman there is my oldest and dearest friend. He was a dear friend of my father's and actually s—"

Stick looked up and shook his head. It was clear he did not want to be recognized as a hero.

"—served with my father in the Army here in Germany. His real name I will not reveal as he doesn't answer to it anyway. We call him 'Stick,' named after the antique controlling stick in his biplane."

"Stick, nice to meet you," said Sigrid. "This is my son, Tomas," pointing to the man standing behind her, "and of course my granddaughter, Sophia. We call her Sophie because she hates Sophia. Says it sounds too Italian and she is German." A small smile crossed her lips.

"So, Stick, what brings you to Germany?" Sigrid asked.

Stick looked at Natalie, who shook her head negatively, and said lightly, "Business. But that is over now and I'll be heading back to the United States sometime tomorrow. It's been an enjoyable experience and, other than the business part, an enjoyable visit. I hope to return sometime in the future, but time will tell."

"Stick, I didn't know you were leaving so soon. Why?" said Natalie.

"Well, if truth be known, I kind of miss the ocean," said Stick. "You know, the sound of the waves, the fresh breeze from the sea, and watching the waves caress the shore. You know, Natalie, you've been there before."

"Indeed, I have," said Natalie. "And I can understand it. We will talk about it more on the ride back to the hotel."

"And the young man sitting next to Stick? "Is he also a friend of yours," asked Sigrid as Sophie's eyes widened waiting for an answer.

"That's John. He is Stick's son. They work together, actually we work together. He is the first graduate of the company's intern program and has done well for himself. He is a good guy."

Sigrid could feel the smile on Sophie's face as she asked, "Are you here for work also?"

"Yes," said John. "We all came over for the same project, but I am going to stay a little bit longer to work at the airport."

Natalie stared at him with a quizzical look. "I didn't know that," she said. "What is going on?"

"Well," said John. "The original intent was to learn the foreign trade business from Dieter, but as you know, the project took up most of our time. I called Dick back at the office and explained what happened and asked for another week. He and Dieter talked and agreed that I could stay another week to learn that part of the business. I figured that as long as I was here, it would be a good opportunity. Hope you don't mind."

"No," said Natalie, "no problem. In fact, good idea." She turned toward Sigrid. "See, that's why is going to go far in his work." Natalie glanced at Sophie and could read the excitement on her face.

"So, John, are you going to have dinner here every night during your stay?"

"I believe so. I need to try Tomas' cooking and the hospitality seems particularly inviting," he said as he looked directly into Sophie's eyes.

She smiled.

Sigrid coughed, more as a distraction than anything else. "And the gentleman sitting next to you Natalie, does he also work for the same company?"

Natalie smiled at the thought. "No, he doesn't. Well, in a sense he does. This is Chris, Chris Palermo. He works for the Governor of New Jersey as a chief advisor. He came as part of the project we were working on to be a conduit between Condor and the Governor."

Sophie's head jerked upwards. "Wait, the news reports were talking about a hijacking of a Condor airplane at Frankfurt. Is that the project you are talking about?"

Natalie lowered her head, berating herself for mentioning Condor. She recovered, raised her eyes, and softly replied, "Yes. We all work for Condor Airlines, well, except for Chris, and came to provide support to the local authorities. It is over now, and we are moving onward."

"The news reports said that the crew was rescued, the plane secured, but that two hijackers were killed in the rescue attempt," said Sophie. "Did you have anything to do with that?"

Natalie looked at Sophie with a stark face. "Directly, no, indirectly probably. We helped design and plan the project but we had no direct contact or killing of anybody. The US Government provided special forces to extradite the airplane crew and we helped them plan the operation. The killing, while regrettable, was necessary to protect the crew members. In fact, the captain of the plane actually subdued the leader of the hostages and prevented him from doing any further damage. She did a heroic job."

"She?" asked Sophie.

"Yes," replied Natalie. "The captain of the airplane was a woman. In fact, all the crew members were women. They represented themselves very well and all are safe and secure now, resting before heading back home. We are all glad about that."

"Absolutely," said Chris. "And I will be heading back home tomorrow also."

"No."

Chris turned his head to look at Natalie. "The project is over; my task is done. I'll be heading home tomorrow with Stick."

"No."

"What do you mean *no*? The Governor needs me."

"No, he doesn't. He can wait another week."

"What do you mean, he can wait another week. You don't know that. I need to talk with him."

"Don't bother, I already did."

"What!! You talked with the Governor? How could you do that, how could you get through all the hoops to talk with him?" said Chris.

"It's amazing how a little talk about re- election support can help smooth the skids. They were all very nice when I introduced myself. The governor himself was very pleasant and gratefully offered another week of your protection for my safety and honor as a gesture of friendship. I, of course, thanked him profusely."

With an aside to Natalie, Chris whispered, "So have you ever given a thought about politics?"

Natalie smiled, and whispered back, "The Governor did mention something about a Lieutenant Governor position being open, but I told him I was too busy to think 'bout that."

Chris looked at Natalie quizzically.

"I did happen to mention that I had a person in mind who would be a great Lieutenant Governor."

With a slight hesitation, Chris asked, "And who would that be?"

"Chris, I'm surprised," Natalie said with a twinkle in her eye. "You know how us politicians are, always talking about openness and transparency, but there are some things we just don't want to talk about. You understand, right?"

Chris starred at her with blank eyes, like the eyes of the wooden lion poised upon the Lowenbrau keg behind the bar. And yet, here was Chris, having stumbled across a facet of the psyche that was Natalie, a dumb genius, a slovenly sophisticate, a villainous hero, a woman he thought he knew, but now the only thing he knew was that he didn't know. Revelations, thou art great!

Chris turned to the table and with a slight nervous laugh said he would be staying another week to "keep Natalie safe and protect her honor." It was his duty.

Sigrid clapped her hands. "Good," she said. "Next week-end, before you leave, we will have a little party here. Tomas can cook, we can drink wine and dance." Sigrid spared a glance at Sophie. "The young ones can entertain themselves. It will be fun."

Light chatter took up the next few minutes as the Americans got ready to leave. Shaking hands all around, some longer than others, they set a time for the party. Sigrid, Tomas, and Sophie waved as the car drove out of the village toward the airport and the hotel.

Natalie leaned over the Chris as he was driving and whispered quietly, "We'll talk about the honor part later, alone."

Chris' wide smile could hardly keep the car on the road.

Chapter Nineteen

The next morning the four Americans drove over to Herr Zink's office. John and Stick said their good-byes to Natalie and Chris. John was going to Dieter's office to learn about international trade and Stick was meeting with the admin assistant to arrange for his flight back home. Meanwhile, Natalie and Chris headed to Dieter's office to extend their thanks and fill him in on their plans for the next week.

"Dieter," said Natalie as they walked into his office, "wanted to thank you for the hospitality and the help in resolving the hostage situation. You and your people did a wonderful job, and we all appreciate it."

Dieter nodded in appreciation and gestured for them to sit down for a minute. "You are welcome," he replied. "I am glad it all worked out. So, what are your plans for the next week? Being the first time in Germany, what is it you are wanting to do, to see?"

"Well," said Natalie, "I want to see Heidelberg. I have heard so much about the city, I want to see it for myself. From there, I am torn between wanting to visit Bavaria, you know, Munich and Garmisch and the middle Rhine area, Koblenz and Koln and the castles along the Rhine. Haven't really decided yet, though Heidelberg for sure."

"Since you are going to Heidelberg let me give you a proposed hotel. It is centrally located, right by the Alte Brucke and the old town area, neat, clean, and has a great restaurant. I'll have my secretary make a reservation for you. I am sure you will like it. Oh, here is a sheet of directions to the hotel I keep available for visitors if they are headed there. It will help you to not get lost."

"Herr Zink, Dieter, thanks again for your help. We appreciate it. We'll be back Friday night as we have a little party on Saturday in Oberstdorf that we must attend with our long-lost family and friends and Sunday we will be going back home. Again, thank you and see you soon!!"

Natalie and Chris left the office, got in the car, and proceeded to head out of town and toward Heidelberg.

The drive was uneventful, unless you consider driving at ninety to one hundred miles per hour down a concrete ribbon while cars behind you are blaring their horns and blinking their lights telling you to get over or get off the road. It was amazing at how fast little Volkswagens could go!

After about thirty minutes of this, the Heidelberg exit loomed ahead, and Chris happily turned off the Autobahn and onto a local highway. A few minutes later they were creeping through the new part of Heidelberg looking for the turn-off shown on the map. A couple of traffic lights later, an obtrusive right ramp led them to a two-lane road that changed everything.

Suddenly they were transformed into a long-lost era. The highway paraded alongside the Neckar River on the left and on the right were buildings belonging to the University of Heidelberg.

"This is the oldest university in Germany, established in 1386, and one of the three oldest universities in Europe," said Natalie turning to Chris.

"How did you know that?" asked Chris. Natalie glanced at him. "I did some research beforehand, to get an idea of what we are seeing. Keep an eye open, we need to turn shortly according to the map."

Just as soon as she spoke, a quick cobblestone ramp appeared on the right. Chris nudged the car onto and up the ramp, putting it near the middle of Old Town Heidelberg and right in front of the Alte Brucke, or Old Bridge, a famous landmark of Heidelberg.

"Dieter said the hotel was near this bridge so find a place to park and we'll look for—oh there it is, just as he said. Hotel zur Alten Brucke. Let's check it out."

Chapter Twenty

The plastic wheels on the suitcases jumped more than rolled on the cobblestones leading to the hotel. The narrow walkway leading to the front was bordered on one side by an old red brick building while on the other side was an outdoor dining area, complete with potted trees surrounding each table, giving it a sense of being outdoors in a park and private.

A stone archway greeted the visitors, and they entered a small courtyard, flanked on either end by a large stone fireplace, with a long banquet table centered in the middle. Opposite the archway were a couple of steps leading to a small office where a man sat pouring over papers and drinking a cup of something. He didn't notice them until they settled their suitcases and walked up the steps to check in.

Glancing up, the man behind the desk rose, smiled, and said, "Ah, Americans."

Natalie and Chris looked over at each other with a wondering glance. "How did you know we were Americans," she asked the man.

"Well, your clothes. No one here in Germany wears clothes like that, we are much more casual with jeans and simple dresses, not to mention the shoes. Who wears patent leather shoes in Germany, and as for heels for the women, nobody wears them around here especially withs the cobblestone streets. One slip and a broken ankle!"

With a quick look at each other, Chris and Natalie immediately understood the man reaction. With a quick smile, they turned back to him. Natalie said, "We are here to check in."

The man nodded and sat down behind his desk to check some papers. "Williams, right?" he said.

Natalie was a bit surprised but answered affirmatively. "How did you know that?" she questioned.

"Dieter, eh, Herr Zink, he called and made the reservation. He asked that I take good care of you upon arrival. I assured him I would do that."

"Do You know Dieter, eh, Herr…" Natalie drifted off, confused as to the pronunciation of the man-behind-the-desk's last name.

The man behind the desk laughed. "No one can ever pronounce my name so don't worry about that. Even after two years in England where I went to school, it's still a mystery to most."

The man stood up, leaned over the desk, and pointed to the name plate sitting at the front of the desk. "See the letter 'T' in front of the last name? That stands for Theodore. Not a very popular name among Germans. As a result, when I was young, I was called Theo. The name has stuck with me for many years and even today I am known as Theo. So, my friends, please call me Theo."

"Well, Theo, thank you for that. But you didn't answer the question. How do you know Dieter."

"Ah," said Theo. "Dieter and his wife have been coming to Heidelberg for many years and they always stay in my hotel. As a result, we have been friends for a long time, and he usually recommends his friends or business associates stay with us when visiting Heidelberg. We appreciate his recommendations and try to meet his needs."

Theo sat down and looked again at his papers. "Dieter wasn't sure how many rooms would be needed. Will that be one room or two?"

"Two," said Chris quickly.

"One," said Natalie.

"Two," said Chris, looking at Natalie.

"One room will suffice, Theo," said Natalie as if giving an order. "We will manage."

Theo looked at Chris who nodded perceptibly in agreement. With a quick annotation, the room was booked, and keys handed over to the two Americans.

"This room is one of our better rooms and the one Dieter likes to occupy every time they visit. It is on the first floor. The elevator is just round the corner, next to the door leading into the breakfast room. I hope you—"

"Wait," said Chris. "Why do we need to take the elevator if the room is on the first floor?"

Theo smiled again. "Well, things are a little different here in Germany. You see, while where you live, the first floor is actually at ground level, here the ground level floor is called 'Grund' or ground. Our first floor is your second floor in your country. It's a little confusing but you'll get used to it."

Both Natalie and Chris nodded in understanding, took the keys, grabbed their bags and walked to the elevator. While small, the elevator was large enough for two people and their luggage. With a lurch and a couple of squeaks, it slowly rose to the first floor and stopped. The couple got out, spotted the room number on the door at the end of the hall and walked toward it. Chris slipped his key into the lock and opened the door.

"Oh my God," he exclaimed as the door swung open and revealed the spacious interior.

Chapter Twenty-One

"What?" said Natalie as she brushed past Chris, looking down to make sure her suitcase wheels made it across the door threshold. "What's the mat—" She stopped in mid-sentence and looked around.

"Oh, wow!!" she exclaimed as her eyes peered around the room.

"How am I going to explain this on my expense account," Chris said.

"Hey, I signed the registration and used my credit card. How am I going to do that?" said Natalie.

Chris smiled. "Well, being the CEO, I am sure you can get it approved," he said as he moved into the room.

They both moved a little further into the room if one could call it that. It was more like a royal anteroom and bedroom combined. Its size dwarfed all the hotel rooms they had ever seen and its opulence was more than the eyes could take.

The room itself took up almost all of the north wing of the hotel. To the right as you entered were two beds. Not ordinary beds, but rather two large queen-sized beds.

And not ordinary queen-sized beds either. They were wrought iron, canopy-covered queen-sized beds draped with a beige eiderdown embroidered with an outline of the Old Bridge and hanging down to the floor on both sides. Four pillows graced the head of each bed, two covered with bright white pillowcases, the size of large European pillows, and two enclosed in shams matching the striking eiderdowns on the beds.

Each bed was lit by a matching gold-plated lamp extending out from the wall above the pillows and the two beds were separated by an antique Louie IV table with its gracious curves and knobs. An antique bench stood at the end of each bed and provided a comfortable place to sit and change.

And to top it off, the beds were raised on a dais, two steps above the floor and rung by a white banister, separating the sleeping area from the rest of the luxurious room.

Stepping down from the dais, the paneled floor was covered with a tan oriental run, speckled with red, green, and yellow designs showing the outline of the Heidelberg castle and a lion, the symbol of the city of Heidelberg.

The other side of the rug, and two steps down from the floor was an oval sitting area. Two sofas, one on each side of the steps, provided plenty of sitting room and faced a large stone fireplace with a marble mantle adorned with fresh flowers and a large mirror above. Two long windows on each side of the fireplace, covered with a thin cotton drape provided privacy while allowing incoming light.

And finally, across the entrance door to these royal accommodations were a pair of French doors, covered also in thin cotton-like material, leading out to an over-sized balcony, fitted with a large metal table and four chairs, allowing for a view of the Old Bridge and the wonderful Neckar River flowing under it while sipping a cup of coffee in the morning, or winding down the day with a wine or cognac before climbing, literary, into bed.

It was a beautiful sight and a glorious room.

"Well," said Chris, "I guess this will do. Let's put things away and tour the city. Which bed do you want?"

Natalie stared at him, and realized he was serious. "I'll take the one on the right. It's closer to the bathroom and I usually get up during the night. It's going to be difficult enough not to fall down the stairs, besides having to locate the bathroom. The one on the right is fine."

In the next couple of minutes, they unpacked, hung things up and walked to the elevator, pushing the down button to the ground floor. As they exited the elevator, Theo was coming out of the breakfast room and almost ran over them.

"Oh," he said, "glad I ran into you. I forgot to tell you about this evening."

"This evening?" Natalie asked.

"Yes, this evening. Three times a year the city of Heidelberg celebrates the destruction of our beloved castle, burned by the French during the Thirty Years War. People travel from all over Europe to witness it. It's quite a spectacular event. Anyway, it was scheduled to occur last night, but the weather, the rain, caused the postponement of the event and the rescheduling of it for this evening. A lot of people were disappointed, but it is a good thing for you as you will be able to experience it. I wanted to let you know so you could enjoy."

"Thanks, Theo," said Chris. "Is there any particular place to go to watch it?"

"Most people, tourists, think that getting as close to the castle as possible is the best way to see it. However, we locals know better. The best place to watch the show is actually further away. In fact, across the Old Bridge."

"Really?" questioned Natalie.

"Absolutely," replied Theo. "Go across the bridge and turn left when you get to the other side. Walk about twenty or thirty meters and there is a grassy knoll on your right. Walk up a couple of steps, spread your blanket, oh I'll leave a blanket for you on the banquet table over there, sit down and enjoy the show. From there you can see the whole of the castle along with the burning of the Old Bridge. Plus, all the boats on the river are lit up in celebration so that is also a treat. In any event, that is the best place to be."

"Great," said Chris. "We are now going to the main square by the church for a little liquid refreshment and a bite to eat. Appreciate the tip and, by the way, the room is acceptable," he said with a wirily grin on his face.

Theo smiled and nodded his head. With a slight wave he moved to the office and the mound of paperwork piled on his desk. Meanwhile, Natalie and Chris walked under the arch and headed to the town square.

Chapter Twenty-Two

The walk to the main square only took a few minutes. Length was not a problem. Cobblestones were. After many years of walking on flat surfaces, the ability to walk safely and securely is severely tested when walking on cobblestones.

Natalie and Chris laughed at each other as they stumbled onward, clinging to each other as the need occurred. Finally reaching the main square they looked upon it with amazement.

Before them was the medieval square, surfaced with those darn cobblestones and centered on a water fountain adding sound to the color.

The square, and it was a square, was bordered by the apse of the ancient church on one side and opposite it stood the Pharmacal Museum, part of the University of Heidelberg, depicting pharmacal work throughout the ages.

The other two sides of the square featured both indoor and outdoor cafes, bakeries, a few hotels, coffee shops, a small convenience store selling mostly wine and spirits, along with a couple of gift shops. A casual, friendly, and congeal atmosphere filled the air surrounding the square and invited visitors to come and sit, enjoy the ambiance, watch the people, and let the world pass them by. That is what Natalie and Chris did.

The middle of the square was populated by metal tables, each seating four patrons and covered with a fancy-colored umbrella, shielding them from the occasional rain, but mostly from the warm sun during the summer months.

While Natalie and Chris searched for an unoccupied table, Chris wondered about the umbrellas. They seemed to be grouped by color. There were red ones, green ones, blue ones, orange ones, and white ones. All together forming a kaleidoscope of colors like a bird's eye view of Monet's *Parisian Café*. It was an experience of a different sort.

Settling on a choice table near the center of the square and situated in a position to view the beautiful castle on the hill overlooking the old city and the square, they began to experience the reason they came to the city.

What immediately captivated them was the castle on the hill. It stood in all its majesty, its red brick and stone exterior extruding the strength and confidence of a protector of the city and the guardian of its people. All this despite the crumbling of the tower. now witness to the follies of war, falling halfway down the hill upon which it was situated.

Chris stared up at the castle, its monumental size overpowering its surroundings. Adding to the grandeur of the castle, a large, exceptionally large, balcony or patio looked out over the old city.

The balcony itself could easily hold over one hundred people with ample room for knights and their horses. It was more of an outdoor grand ballroom than a balcony and was a favorite spot of the many tourists who visited the castle.

Natalie noticed Chris' attention to the castle. "It's beautiful, isn't it?" she said with the hope of getting a response.

"Yes, it is," said Chris. "Beautiful, majestic, and nowadays, sad."

"Sad? Why sad?"

"Sad because of all it's been through. But sad now, because of the way it's being treated."

"Why do you say that?" said a confused Natalie. "How is it being treated badly?"

Chris turned to look at Natalie, a little confused as to why she did not see the same things he did.

"Look," said Chris as if talking to himself. "Look at all those people on the balcony. They gather around the stone railing of the thing, all the more to be able to look down at the city while making sure the f-stop on their cameras are correctly set to show the pictures to the folks back home. And all the while, the significance, the importance, the history of the fabled castle are right behind them, encased in the bricks that make up the stories, the history, the loves, the romances, even the duals and fights, that occurred right where they are standing. And yet they are forgotten, or even worse, not even thought of. It is as though the castle magically appeared one day from which to take pictures rather than the home that people loved, yes maybe kings and queens, probably more like dukes and duchess but nevertheless, people who lived their everyday lives within its walls, walked its gardens, sang and danced in its open courtyard and balcony, and whose lives were intimately bonded to its presence. It is just sad.”

Natalie looked at him as she had never looked at anyone else before. Here he had opened himself to her, not asking her to understand, not asking for her to agree, just asking her to listen.

And she did, with the wanting to hear more.

“Can I get you something?” asked the waitress.

Chapter Twenty-Three

Chris looked up. "Oh yes," he said. "A glass of Merlot and a beer, please," looking over to Natalie and getting her approving nod concerning the wine-type. She sat there quietly, her chin resting on her two hands which were propped up by her elbows on the table, staring intently at Chris.

"Large or small beer," asked the server.

"Wait. Wait," said Chris. "I come all this way to Germany and all I hear is people speaking English. How come?"

The server laughed. "Well, for the most part, all students in Germany are required to learn English. The older folks not so much as they tend to shy away from English and stick with German. The younger people, like me, and especially those who deal with the tourists, speak English. Besides that, I am from Pennsylvania, so English is my native tongue," she laughed.

"Now I understand and thank you for the explanation. Explains a lot."

Chris looked at Natalie and started to say something. Abruptly he stopped, tilted his head slightly and asked, "What, what's the matter?"

Natalie raised her head and shook her head. "Nothing is the matter; I had never heard you speak like that."

"You mean the way I talked to the server?"

"No, the way you talked about and described the castle. I had never seen that side of you before."

"Oh well, we're on vacation now and I can be a little more open with my thoughts."

"I like it," said Natalie. "We're your parents as expressive as that?"

"No, not at all. Especially my father. He was an engineer and wanted me to be an engineer also. I was obligated to take engineering courses because he was footing the bill. So mechanical engineering, electrical engineering, architecture engineering, anything that ended in engineering was fine with him. I was even able to get by with political science because science was in the title."

"My mother, on the other hand, wanted me to be as well rounded as possible and encouraged me to use my available electives to try different things. I enjoyed that, away from math and science, and using the right side of my brain a little bit more. Hell, I even took an art class in the hope it would improve my mechanical drawing. But abstract mechanical drawing is not readily accepted," as he laughed.

She smiled an encouraging smile, as if urging him to go on. And on he did.

"Let me tell you a little story about one of my adventures. I was taking this art class, and we were learning about all the renowned artists, their techniques, their subjects, their trials, and tribulations, and ultimately their successes. It was really interesting, hearing and learning about the behind-the-scenes events which shaped their lives and thus their works. I enjoyed it.

"One day I was thumbing a magazine, don't recall which one, but came upon an article about furniture and what not. Not something I really enjoyed but I spotted above the sofa a picture that interested me. It was pretty modern, not something any of the well-known artists would do. It consisted of a stark white canvas with a black and chrome frame and on it was a Chinese figure of a vocabulary symbol painted in simple, dark black paint. Pure and simple, yet it stood out to me. Don't know why, but it did. So, like a fool, I decided that I could do that and proceeded down that path.

"Over the next couple of days I found an art shop and bought a large white canvas already stretched over a wooden frame. I figured large was better than small and it would fit over my sofa. The next day I went to a hardware store and bought a can of black paint and a paint brush, about the size used to do the trim on a house. I was all ready to begin my art career!!!

"When the weekend came, I took my new-found tools down to the basement and proceeded to create my first masterpiece. With a couple of broad strokes of the brush, a couple of dots, and the swirl of the brush, I was done. I had done it and was filled with pride of accomplishment. However, when I compared my creation with that in the picture, they were in no way comparable. Mine lacked the intensity one could feel in the picture. It lacked the compassion that flashed back from the picture. It simply lacked.

"But not to be outdone, I took the now screwed up white canvas to a frame shop and had the identical frame made from the picture. I picked up the finished product a week and went home, hung it over the couch and stood back with a feeling of success.

"That is until a friend of mine came over and asked what the hell was that thing hanging over my couch. I looked at him, looked at the picture, looked back at him, and again the picture. Without a word I took the picture down, put it in a closet, and never mentioned it again. Such was my foray into creative art."

Natalie laughed and reached out for his hand. She squeezed it tight and giggled like a little girl who had just found a secret. Chris laughed at himself and squeezed back.

And they talked for the next couple of hours, until the sun set, and the streetlights blinked on.

"We had better get going before there is no room at the knoll," borrowing a well-known phrase.

"Oh, that's bad," she said with a groan. "But you're right. Let's go."

Chris left some money on the table for the server, and they started down the uneven street, her holding his arm for stability and he enjoying the contact. When they were even with the hotel, Chris went into the courtyard and captured the blanket Theo had left for them. Arm in arm, they continued past the bronze monkey, through the twin towers, and over the bridge to the other side. Turning left, they walked a couple of meters and immediately spotted the knoll, dotted with a few other couples. Leading the way, Chris found a spot to unfold the blanket and set it on the grass, still a little wet from the rain the night before. He sat down and motioned Natalie to do the same. She turned around facing the river and started to sit down. Suddenly, her shoes slipped on the wet grass, and she started falling quickly to the ground. Without hesitation, Chris reached up and grabbed her hips with both hands and guided her gently down. She looked at him and said, "That was nice. Thank you."

"Welcome," said Chris. "We'll have to do it again sometime."

They both laughed.

Chapter Twenty-Four

The large tourist boats moved silently into position, as close to the Old Bridge as the authorities would allow, to afford their customers the best view possible of the old castle. Privately owned yachts creeped past them into a position closer to the shore, dropped their anchors and settled in for an evening's entertainment followed by some cold beer and a schnapps or two. It was all in a day's work.

Natalie and Chris watched the diorama unfold before them, smiling as each boat secured its final watery location, waiting for the show to begin.

Several other couples joined them on the knoll, each nodding knowing they had arrived at the best place. Little kids anxiously sat among their parents, asking incessantly when the fireworks were to begin. And as parents are wont to do, they responded, "Pretty soon."

The intensity of the watch built up as the last remaining rays of the sun disappeared behind the hills surrounding the old city. One by one, the streetlights dimmed, raising the hopes of the viewers, waiting for the first sign of the show. And then it began.

A single rocket screeched into the sky above the castle leaving behind a trail of flame and smoke. Reaching its peak, the rocket exploded with a loud bang like that of cannon, sending its contents into the sky and scattering them forming the sides of an umbrella, The flakes of shiny metal slowly floated toward the castle, their tiny fluorescent flames illuminating the now dark sky as they approached their final fate.

As if on cue, the whole scene erupted in fiery interruption of the final assault on the castle. Flames leapt from the base of the walls, their gold and red colors mixing into colorful reminders of the fateful day. Rockets raced across the ramparts of the castle, some screaming their way while others seemed to stop, dropping more burning flakes to the castle courtyard and the walls still standing. Alternating lights of red, green, and gold burst upon the red brick structure followed by more fireworks dashing against the walls. Sounds from the hidden speakers mimicked cannons firing, shells exploding, and firearms shooting. It was a wonderful sight and took one away from the moment.

But that also was shattered as the epic battle soon consumed the Old Bridge. Natalie and Chris shuddered unexpectedly as the shooting flames of the flood lights, combined with the sounds and fury of the fireworks, suddenly overcame them, causing them to shy away from the bridge they had come to love.

The realization that the sounds of destruction were only a symbolic representation of the past, they eased back to the blanket and watched the castle burn, occasionally glancing at the bridge to make sure it still was there.

And with a final rocket above the castle, a final explosion, and the final release of thousands of metal shreds, colored in the hues of the German flag, the wonderous show ended.

Seemingly exhausted, as though they had fought the battle, the pair exhaled their withheld breath and expressed a sigh of relief. They looked at each other and laughed at the knowledge that they had both experienced the same thing and reacted the same.

"Let's go," said Natalie.

"Let the others leave first. We're in no hurry."

They sat back down and watched as the others left, as the boats lifted their anchors and headed back to their moorings and docks, and the smoke cleared from both the castle and bridge. Authorities searched the bridge for unexploded fireworks, moving from one watery pier to another till all was clear.

"OK, let's go," said Chris. "We've avoided most of the crowds on this side of the river, though the other side still looks pretty packed." He got up and held out a hand to help Natalie up without slipping. A minute later, they were walking across the Old Bridge wondering what to do.

Suddenly Natalie stopped. "Wait, before we leave the Bridge, I want to check out something I saw when crossing over it. It's on the side of the tower, by the hotel."

"I know what it is," he said with a grin on his face.

"What?" she asked, hands on hips and a look of defiance on her face. "What?"

"The Monkey."

"How did you know it was the monkey," she asked, bewildered by his answer.

"I saw you look at it when we walked past and hesitate. Figured you would want to check it out."

"OK, wise guy. I supposed you know all about it too."

"Well, not all, but some. It is amazing what you can learn just by reading."

As they approached the end of the Bridge, a small crowd could be seen walking away from the statue. The pair rounded the corner and stood in front of the figure.

"So, tell me 'bout this thing."

Chris smiled and began to reveal what he read. "It is actually a replica of an older statue that stood at the opposite end of the Bridge back in the early days, I mean like in the 1500's. It was destroyed during one of the many wars during that period. Remember at that time, this Old Bridge was the only way across the river and into the town, so the monkey was a welcoming sign to friends and a warning sign to enemies. It was commissioned in 1970's and put on this side of the river as a reminder of that and as a tourist attraction. Notice the two hands of the monkey?"

"Yea, I was wondering what they represented," said Natalie.

"According to the article I read in the hotel room as you were getting changed, the two hands represent good things. The left hand holds a couple of horns, what of I'm not so sure, but the story is that if you touch them, or hold them, you will, sometime in the future, return to Heidelberg. As for the right hand, again the story is that touching it or holding on to it will bring you great wealth. Again, reading does wonders."

Natalie looked at Chris in amazement. She smiled, reached out, and grabbed both hands of the monkey. "I really do what to come back here some day and spend more time among the locals. That would be wonderful. And as for the wealth, everyone wants more wealth, so why not me?"

Chris frowned a little. "Wait, you want wealth? You're the CEO of one of the largest airlines in the world and draw a hefty salary. You are also the holder of a majority of the stock, which means you get a huge dividend each year one is declared. And I don't remember Condor Airlines never declaring a dividend. What more money could you possibly want?"

Natalie looked at him with an all-knowing smile.

"Who says I was talking about money?"

An imaginary clap of thunder roared through the sky.

Chris just stared, then spoke, "Would you like to get a glass of wine and watch the world go by?"

"You know," said Natalie, "it's been a long day and I'm tired. Let's just go back to the room and get a good night's sleep. I figure we have a long day tomorrow, with all we want to see, and could use the rest."

Chris nodded and they walked back to the hotel from the Bridge, took the rickety elevator up one floor and entered the royal bedchamber, as they called it.

Without asking, he walked to the bar, selected a bottle of local wine and poured two glasses. He offered one to Natalie and they both moved to the balcony to watch the city call it a night, and dream of the day to come.

"Well, that's enough for me," said Natalie. "I'm going to get changed and climb into bed. I've got the one nearest the bathroom, right?"

Chris nodded. "I'll be in mine by the time you get done. See you in the morning."

She nodded, grabbed her stuff, and walked into the bathroom, shutting the door behind her. He looked as she did so, finished his wine and went to get changed.

He left the French doors open to get fresh air during the night and perhaps even hear the river water floating past. While usually sleeping in the nude, he figured discretion was in order and left his shorts on, crawling into bed and pulling the sheet and blanket over himself.

Natalie came out of the bathroom, her silhouette outlined by the bathroom light. She wore a long, silky nightgown, thick enough to deter any peeping toms while flattering her waist and shaping her hips. She moved between the beds and climbed into hers, and with a "good night," she turned off the overhead light and got settled.

Chris figured that was the end of the evening and positioned himself in his favorite sleeping position, laying on his right side, facing the French doors, his head resting on his right arm which stretched out to grab the pole of the canopy bed.

His left arm settled on his hip, his elbow bent, and his left hand pushing the mattress, providing stability to the whole body. His legs bent into a near-fetal position, and he readied himself for a good night's sleep and a busy day ahead.

Fifteen minutes later he felt a sag in his mattress and the rustling of his covers. Almost immediately, a pair of smooth legs lined themselves up with his, and tiny knees nestled into the crook created by his bent legs.

Cautiously he asked, "What is this?"

A childish voice answered. "This is how my dog and I sleep at home. I do better this way. Hope you don't mind?"

Chris mind raced through a thousand scenarios in the matter of five seconds. From doing nothing to grabbing her and kissing her and all other thoughts in-between. Finally, after what seemed like hours, he breathed a sigh of resignation, said, "Fine." He closed his eyes.

Five minutes later a soft hand of five fingers touched his elbow and slowly moved up his arm, eventually coming to rest on his shoulder. He reached up and patted her arm and with a genuine sigh of contentment, whispered, "Fine." And no one could see the smile on his face.

Chapter Twenty-Five

It was not the seeping of the morning sunlight through the open French door, nor the sounds of the trucks making their early morning deliveries to the restaurants and shops on the streets and alleys below that roused him.

Rather it was the sound of water splashing from the shower on the other side of the bathroom door, a sound he had not heard in quite a while, and which wrestled a smile from his still slumbering face.

Chris threw his legs out from under the sheets, rolled over, and steadied himself on the floor before attacking the day. His first opponent, the coffee pot, surrendered with little fight and he turned to welcome the next twenty-four hours from the balcony, coffee cup in hand, and wondering when she would be done.

And as wishes sometimes are granted, the bathroom door opened and there she stood, wrapped in a white terry-cloth bathrobe provided by the hotel, waving a hair dryer in one hand and a hairbrush in the other. "Good morning," she said with a smile.

"Morning," he replied saluting her with his coffee cup. "Want some?"

"Nope, I'll wait till we go downstairs to breakfast. Don't want to fill up before that."

"Ugh, breakfast," he said. "I am tired of the same old breakfast all the time. Ever since we came to Germany and stayed in the American-style hotel, it was the same thing—eggs, bacon or sausage, toast or English muffin, perhaps some fried potatoes, and a choice of two juices. Not much variety there. I'll wait till we can find a local bakery and indulge myself."

"OK, suit yourself, but the German breakfasts are legendary, and I am looking forward to seeing for myself. Oh, I'll be done here in about ten minutes and then you can do your thing. After that, we can check out the hotel cupboard and see what they have for the mice."

He laughed and waited his turn.

They exited the elevator and walked into the breakfast room, rather they walked into a cornucopia of breakfast items. Two shelves on each side of the entrance highlighted the endless variety of foodstuffs available, from several diverse kinds of fruit like bananas, apples, oranges, slices of cantaloupe, and even mangos to cereal in glass containers, each with its own scoop, to little packages of familiar brands.

Little bowls of raisins, nuts, crackers, and other toppings dotted the shelves. A large container of ice housed pitchers of juices, orange and apple, and milk for the cereal. At the end of the shelf was a large shiny urn full of coffee, with cups and saucers standing by.

The other two shelves are what made the difference. First, there were slices of meats, salami, ham, prosciutto, bologna, and a stick of peperoni to be sliced as one wished. Next to that was a large board stacked with all kinds of cheeses, gouda, brie, Swiss, cheddar, and some others which had not been named.

Condiments scattered around the food provided toppings as needed. But near the end of the shelve was the bread, the German bread. There must have been five or six assorted styles of bread from hard and soft rolls to banquettes and creosotes.

Hard rye bread and even cheese bread added to the selections and completing the feast were pastries and cookies, some filled with jelly, some with nuts, but all looking like they came out of a professional cookbook.

And finally standing behind the meat and cheese offerings, a chef offered his services to fix eggs as you wanted. While hard-boiled eggs were abundant on the shelves, eggs over-easy, scrambled, poached, and even omelets were made to order.

It easily outclassed the typical American breakfast and to top it off, a patron could return to the shelves as many times as they wish while servers replenished the coffee and juices as needed.

An hour later, and with a huge sigh of relief, breakfast was done. With one last sip of coffee, Natalie asked, "Well, what's next?"

Chris looked bewildered and said, "We had talked about seeing the countryside, let's ask Theo what is around that we might like."

With a nod, they got up, waddled through the breakfast door over to the office to ask for advice.

Chris maneuvered the car out of Heidelberg onto the local two-lane highway and into the countryside. "Where are we going?" he asked Natalie.

"Well, Theo said we should go to Rothenberg, about an hour away. He gave us some information on the place and a map to get us there. It seems pretty interesting.

"The town is surrounded by an intact city wall, which protected the place during the medieval period. In fact, according to the brochure, it was one of the ten largest cities in Europe during that time and was declared an Imperial Free City, which meant it only answered to the head of the Holy Roman Empire. Sounds like a major place."

"What's it called again," asked Chris.

"Rothenberg. Rothenberg ob der Tauber. Apparently, there is a river called the Tauber and the city was built on it."

"OK, well, Rothenberg, here we come!"

About an hour and a half, two wrong turns, numerous horn soundings, and one U-turn, they arrived at the entrance to the old town of Rothenberg. And it was as if the world had stood still hundreds of years earlier.

The cobblestone roadway led directly to the city gate which opened between two large stone gatehouses, a metal grate suspended above the road as though ready to drop at a moment's notice.

They stopped car alongside the short road and let their minds wander back several hundred years ago, watching the peasants pulling their carts to the town square to sell their wares, and perhaps the nobility exiting the city for an afternoon ride in the surrounding woods, the woods now blemished with apartments, shops, and gas stations. Keeping the old images in mind, they slowly drove through the gate and into the past.

Stone houses lined the way, each sharing a wall with their neighbor. A parking sign directed them to the right, and they headed directly toward the city wall, its ramparts still standing with a wooden walkway behind the wall allowing protectors to move from position to position without being exposed to searching arrows or spears.

A left turn enabled them to parallel the wall, which had been standing for hundreds of years, and imagine all it had experienced. Further down, a large parking area appeared, and they settled their steed into the first available stall, paid the metal horse-tender its fee, and started walking the cobblestone streets toward the town square.

The town square was the classic medieval square pictured in books and movies, with the largest building being the town hall, a large clock built into the tower of another large building housing the various guilds, and a large open area, paved with more cobblestones to allow for the venders to display their fruits or vegetables or their freshly killed and cured meat. Carpenters showed their home-made items made from various trees and minstrels and musicians plied their trade for a few pence.

The beauty of the town to Chris and Natalie was not the actual town itself, though its medieval architecture was understated. The beauty of the town was the idea and thoughts that you were sitting, standing, walking, where others had done the same hundreds of years ago.

That where you sat savoring the beer and wine from the café behind your table, little children once played whatever games they played during that time, running, screaming, laughing, and teasing. It was these thoughts that made the town enjoyable. It was as though the whole town was a backdrop to the thoughts of knights and ladies and the chivalry of the times.

It was this that made the town such a pleasant place to visit. Not to mention the numerous ice cream shops, the traditional German souvenir shops and the inevitable Kathe Wohlfahrt Christmas shops selling decorations year-round. It all made for a nice afternoon.

Natalie glanced over at Chris and saw him deep in thought, kind of staring straight ahead, oblivious to the going-ons around him.

"You all right?" she asked with a worried look on her face.

"Yes," he responded absent-mindedly. "Just thinking."

"Oh, and what would you be thinking about?"

"About last night. I was thinking about last night and us being together."

"Yes," she said, smiling broadly. "It was kind of wonderful, wasn't it?"

"Truly, it was. So wonderful, I almost jumped."

"Jumped?" she quizzed. "What do you mean 'jumped'?"

"You know, jumped, like jumped into love. That kind of jumped."

"Excuse me for being a little presumptuous, but do you mean 'fell in love'?" she asked.

Chris turned his head and looked right into her eyes. "No, not fell in love, jumped into love. There is no falling, at least in my mind."

"I do not understand. People fall in love every day. What is wrong with that?"

"Nothing wrong with it, it's just not accurate, that's all. When one jumps into love there is no falling. See, falling has a negative connation. One falls into the mud, falls into the river, falls over a cliff, falls on the sidewalk, and falls by the wayside. There is no intention there. It is just something that happens, and while that may seem romantic, the same person struggles to get out of the mud, to climb out of the river, to hope to grab onto something to stop the fall over the cliff, and to get up from the wayside and continue moving. Falling lacks the intent of the person experiencing the fall, and maybe that is where the phrase 'love conquers all' comes from. But the truth is that without the intent, without the desire, love is doomed to failure."

"And," he continued, "that is where 'jumping' comes in. You see, jumping is a positive effort. It is not arbitrary. It is something desirous and wanting to happen. And by wanting it to happen, instead of it accidentally happening, it is stronger, able to withstand assaults of any nature, and willing to fight to protect itself. Like the walls around this city. They did not fall into place. They were deliberately built; they were jumped into place. And last night, I almost jumped and only one thing kept me from doing so."

Intrigued, Natalie whispered quietly, "And what was that?"

With a glance that opened his soul, he answered, "You, I need, I desperately need, to know who you are."

Natalie leaned back into her chair with a slight frown and a wondering look. "What do you mean? We have been seeing each other for months now. We have shared some good times, and occasionally some not-so-good times. But we have endured them all and still have stayed together. I don't understand the statement that you don't know who I am. How can that be?"

Chris smiled like a Chesire cat. "Oh, perhaps I misspoke. I know who you are. I've read your resume, I have seen press releases from your people extolling Condor's accomplishments and always mentioning your name, I have read and seen magazine articles about you and the company and, again, its accomplishments. I have done all that. So, I know all that. I have also seen you in negotiations with competitors, head-to-head, and almost always achieving your goals after beating the other side of the table about the head and shoulders till they concede, and yet, and yet, ten minutes later the two sides walk out of the room as though they are best friends. I don't understand. So maybe the question is not 'who are you' but rather 'how did you get to be what you are?' Is that a more reasonable question?"

Natalie breathed a sigh of relief, the tension of the moment slipping silently away from her body, her brain telling her that all is all right between them and all he was looking for was assurance that his assessment of her as a being, as a lover, as a partner in life, was accurate, and built to withstand life's pressures. She smiled. I can do that, she thought.

"So," said Natalie. "You are not questioning who I am, you are wondering how I got to where I am, right?"

"Yep," said Chris. "And I'll give you ten minutes to start explaining," with a huge grin on his face.

Startled, Nicole shot back. "Wait, I know doctors who get paid hundreds of dollars an hour to sit with a client for forty-five minutes just to go over one point in their life and you want me to analyze my whole being in ten minutes? Is that what you want?"

"Yep. And you better get started. It's nine minutes now," he said with a chuckle.

She looked at him with this unbelievable face of wonder. But getting the intent of his question she suggested that since it was getting dark, they head back to Heidelberg and they could continue the conversation in the car.

Walking along the cobblestone streets to the parking lot, their hands fell together, or rather, jumped together, and like little kids they waited for the next installment.

Chapter Twenty-Six

Chris slowly drove the car back alongside the town's walls and through the massive gatehouses, leaving one thousands of years behind and entering the world of today. He soon encountered a two-lane highway on the city's outskirts and headed back to Heidelberg.

"So, have you thought about what I asked?"

Natalie thought for a minute. "I did. And I amazed myself at what I realized. All this time I thought it was just me, just who I was, no one else. But that is not the case. I suddenly began to realize that I was them, that they who came before me had such an impact on who I am today. It was truly eye-opening, or perhaps more heart-opening. Let me try and answer your question."

"As you know, my mother and grandfather emigrated to America during the time of the Berlin Blockade. While my grandfather swore that it was because of the fear of another war, after having gone through two of them, I believe that it was because of my mother being pregnant and unmarried. In the little village where they had lived that was a shameful act and I believe my grandfather did not want to face up to it. So, he moved, first to France, then to America and settled in a small German community in the mid-west. His story, and my mother's story, was that my father had died in a plane crash during the blockade. They believed that, though no prove existed either way."

"Things were tough for them, settling in a new place. My grandfather worked wherever he could, and my mother worked cleaning houses for others. But despite that, my grandfather had a dream, a dream of opening a restaurant, or Gasthaus as he had in Germany. He worked hard, saved what he could, and eventually realized that dream and opened a small Gasthaus which was welcomed in the German community. Eventually it became popular among the townspeople and grew. Soon my mother quit her house-cleaning work and started working at the restaurant, just as she had in Germany. It had been a hard struggle, but they had achieved what they wanted.”

“And from that, thinking back on it, I learned about the need for making goals, planning ahead, and looking toward the future. This is a part of me that exists today. If you don’t have a goal, any road will take you there. And that is not acceptable.”

“And a second thing I learned was that you have to work to achieve your goal. nothing in this world is given, nothing is fair, nothing is equal.”

“Well,” she said with a smile. “One thing is equal. Death. Death is equal. Everyone has one. But that is a different story.”

“I heard a lecture once a long time ago about kids when they start out in life after all the preparation and schooling. They enter the working world and the first thing they see is the huge successes that people have. The peak of the mountain. And here they stand at the bottom of the mountain, and all they see is the peak. What they fail to see is the mountain, the path they must take, the work they must put in, the effort they need to expend to reach that peak. So, they start their journey. At first, it’s pretty easy but the higher up the mountain you go, the steeper the incline and the more difficult the task. Eventually they decide they don’t want to climb any more, and they settle for where they are. The peak is still there. They can still see it. But they don’t want to work anymore to get there. So, they settle, make up some excuses as to why it is unreachable, why it is not worth the effort, or the fact that they are happy where they are. And life goes on.”

“Well, I gleaned from watching others and listening to that lecture, that if you are to reach the peak, reach the goal you set for yourself, you have to be willing to exert the effort to reach it. There are no excuses for not trying. Oh, there are circumstances which may prevent your achieving your goal, but they should not be our own doing. So, the lesson is, be willing to work to achieve what you want.”

She sighed. “Setting the goal and be willing to work to get there are two of the most important things that are an integral part of me.”

Natalie looked at Chris as his eyes monitored the road but his ears and his brain monitored her words. With a shrug of her shoulders, she said, “I’m sorry, but you asked the question. Now you must listen to the answers.”

"Thinking back to my early working days, I learned a couple of other things. My first job after college was as an intern at a large company in New Brunswick. It was a meaningless job, but a chance to get my foot into the door. At that time, I had no idea what I wanted to do nor what goal I wanted to achieve. I just wanted to learn the ways of business and this was a good opportunity.

"My first boss was a department head. He had been there for a good length of time and thought he knew everything there was to know about his role and the role of his department. My job was to help others with projects they were tasked with doing so I went from one employee to another as needed. It was a valuable experience. But most of all, I got to witness the management style of the department head. Well, style is a kind word. Slavery is probably more accurate. He ruled the department with an iron head and since he knew it all, he had no regrets in berating his employees for making a mistake. And worst of all, he would humiliate them in front of the others. They were not happy, and if not for the paycheck, they would have left. After working for him for four months there was a relief.

"He got fired. Well, maybe not fired, but at least moved from his position and out of sight. And his replacement arrived.

"I learned more about managing people, working with people who work for you and with you in the remaining two months than the four months prior. The atmosphere in the office completely turned around. It was amazing.

"I remember the first day he arrived. He walked around the department and introduced himself, sat down next to the desks and asked them what they were working on. The employees were stunned and quite honestly, were quiet. They didn't know what to think. That afternoon he called an employee meeting in the large conference room so everyone could have a seat.

"It was quiet in the conference room when he entered and stood at the end of the table. He glanced around, smiled, and introduced himself. Sitting down, he went on to tell his people his work history, where he had worked, what he had done, and why he came to this company. And at the end, and I will never forget this, he asked everyone around the table to introduce themselves and answer the following question. 'Outside of work, what is it that you like to do, and why do you like to do it?'"

She smiled. "Does that sound familiar?"

One of the attendees sitting at the table asked why they were posed the question. The answer surprised them as it was something they had not realized.

"Well," he said. "Let's take a look at your normal day. You get up in the morning, have whatever you have for breakfast, or nothing at all, get into your mode of getting to work, spend eight or nine hours here among the people in this room, make your way back home, stopping as needed or wanted, spend the next four or five hours with your wife and kids, or your TV, and then go to bed. So where did you spend most of your time? Right here in the office, among the people you are sitting across at this moment. Wouldn't it be nice to know something about them, to know their hobbies, what they like and don't like, how they spend their leisure time? Wouldn't that be interesting? That, kind sir, is why I ask you to get to know each other better. And, no, it was not a planted question. It was a normal question and I ask each of you to consider it and learn more about your fellow workers. It makes life easier and the eight hours you spend with them more bearable."

"And that," said Natalie, "is the reason I want to know the people that work for me, and for whom I work. It is an important lesson to be practiced throughout life and is why, after a tough negotiation session, I walk out with the competitor, not as a competitor but as a human being interested in others. It's worked for me and I will keep doing it."

Natalie looked at Chris. His attention was clearly on what she was saying, nodding every so often, smiling more so.

She asked him, "What do you think about that ten-minute analysis?"

Responding quickly, Chris said, "I think I'm glad I only gave you ten minutes," as he pulled into an empty parking space by the hotel. "I also think I need a cold beer and a warm pretzel to simmer the thoughts going through my head."

Natalie nodded, opened the car door and said, "Let's go."

Chapter Twenty-Seven

The tables and chairs outside of Vetter's Brewery were not the most comfortable in the world, but they presented an unprecedented view of Heidelberg walking past. Chris and Natalie sat in their chairs, the table in front of them littered with the remains of their dinner.

A large stein once holding local German beer stood empty in front of Chris and not one, but two empty glasses of wine graced Natalie's presence. Add to that the remains of a salted pretzel and two bowls of goulash soup, and you have proof of well satisfied customers. And they were.

Conversation during the dinner ranged from commenting on the people walking by flaunting their individuality with various fashions or, in some cases, non-fashions, to reflecting on the town they had seen that day and marveling at the fact that it was over one thousand years old, as proven in several written accounts of its importance.

It was hard to believe they had walked on the same ground that knights and lords and ladies had walked and visited farmers selling their fruits and vegetables. It was hard to imagine.

They had barely touched on the conversation which had taken place in the car, nor of the growing attachment that seemed to draw them to each other. Neither wanted to bring it up in fear that doing so would embarrass the other or that they had misinterpreted the happenings.

"Chris," said Natalie.

"Yes?" Chris replied.

"I know you like to sit and watch the world go by, and I enjoy it too. But I feel as though I have been around three times already today and would like a rest. Can we stop for the day?"

"Sure," said Chris. He called the waiter over and paid the check, leaving a tip which was uncalled for as, in Germany, the tip is already included in the price. He didn't care. The service was good.

They walked back to the hotel, stumbling on the never-ending cobblestones, rode the rickety elevator up one floor and entered the sanctuary of their hotel room.

"I'm going to bed," said Natalie. "You can stay up and watch the world all you want," a slight grin on her face.

"Nah, a good night's sleep will do us both good. Go ahead and get changed. I'll turn your bed down and climb into mine. I'll leave the lights on till you're settled."

Natalie grabbed her nightgown and went into the bedroom. Chris turned down her bed and got undressed, leaving his shorts on as he had done the night before. It was a little uncomfortable, as he usually slept naked, but he would deal with it.

Done with his chores, he pulled the covers back, climbed into bed and assumed his normal position, lying on his right side, his right arm stretched out with his head resting on his arm and his legs in their usual semi-fetal position.

Natalie came out of the bathroom, walked between the two beds, and without batting an eye, turned the lights out and climbed into bed beside Chris. Her knees nestled against Chris' as though this was where they belonged. Her hand reached out for his elbow and started moving toward his shoulder. He sighed contentedly and began to doze off.

As though her hand had received a course change, it moved down to his chest and began to trace little circles, little circles, alternating between the softness of her fingertips and the edge of her nails. Like a cross between the softness of rose petals and the sharpness of a knife. The circles got smaller and smaller and slowly moved down his chest and to his abdomen with little to no hesitation. He flinched.

Chris eyes slowly opened as he wondered what was going on. With a little tilt of his neck, he peered over his shoulder and stared right into Natalie's eyes. "What are you doing?" he said.

With a look of solemn honesty, she replied, "Jumping."

There was a hesitation between the two of them as they searched for the right words to say. Neither knew the answer. They only knew what they wanted.

Chris suddenly turned over on his back and said softly to her, "Here, let me give you a hand with that," and swiftly slid his shorts down over his legs and to the bottom of the bed. And with a slight grin, Natalie's circles moved lower and lower and evolved from their beginning form into stroking and caressing. Chris gasped as he realized what was happening and settled back into the depths of the mattress. "Bring it on," he thought.

A couple of minutes later, Chris' abdomen and stomach muscles began to contract and release, a sure indication that whatever she was doing was having an effect. She watched eyes, closely scrutinizing every movement, every reaction. as the end approached closer and closer.

At just the right moment, she raised her body up on her knees and ripped the nightgown off over her head and with the same movement laid her now naked body completely on top of Chris, her soft breasts pressing hard against his chest and her lips searching for his.

Chris' eyes opened wide as Natalie smiled and said, "Here, let me give you a hand with that." And with that, she slid her soft form down his frame, her hot body slowly engulfing him inch by inch by inch until the only thing separating them was lust.

In a whispering raspy voice Natalie spoke anxiously into his ear. "OK, now it's your turn!"

An uncontrollable "oh" and "ah" escaped from her quivering lips as his hips began to move.

***

Two naked bodies lay under the cover of a rumpled white sheet allowing for their bodies to cool down, aided by the breeze generated by an antique fan hanging from the ceiling. Neither party looked at another, they didn't have to with their legs touching each other and their intertwined fingers making love.

Natalie, her eyes softly closed, murmured under her breath, "I wish it would never end. Never end."

Chris looked over at the angelic face and smiled. With a quick move, he straddled her lithe body and pulled her hands up over her head. She looked startled but surprisingly amused while her eyes signaled "go ahead."

He slowly with a free hand swept a wisp of hair from her forehead and lowered his lips, kissing her softly and erasing the questioning frowns from her brow. As if by magic, the lips moved down over the bridge of her nose and settled on her lips, his tongue searching in vain for a dance partner.

Finding none, his tongue traced a path from her lips, down under her chin, along the neck and between two luscious breasts, only stopping to kiss each nipple so they would not feel left out. Continuing downward, the tongue left a moist trail cautiously stopping at the circular belly button.

Chris looked up at Natalie and saw her closed eyes, her clenched mouth, and her two hands still above her head, grasping onto her pillow as though holding on for dear life. Her mouth was slightly open, her breath coming in gasps, as if her whole being was anticipating the painful pleasure soon to coarse through her very soul. He continued.

The tongue moved downward stopping only at the gate to paradise as two hands grasped the sides of his head. His eyes raised upward as Natalie softly spoke. "Don't. Don't. Please don't. Please don't stop. Don't stop, ever. And ever. And ever."

And he heeded her command.

Chapter Twenty-Eight

The tinny chime from the clock on the fireplace mantle struck nine. Chris looked at his watch and confirmed it. "It's time," he thought. "Yep, for her to get up," as he walked over to the bed. "Natalie, it's time to get up."

"No," came the sharp retort from under the covers.

"Yes, it is. We have a lot to do today and need to get started."

"I don't wanna," came the whining response.

"Come on now, let's get going."

"I don't want to. Go away."

Chris thought for a minute then walked over to the breakfast tray bought to the room by the dining room staff and poured himself another cup of coffee. Taking a sip, he poured a second cup and walked back to the bed with it. In one smooth motion he raised a corner of the eiderdown, slipped the cup of coffee under, and let the aroma of the fresh-brewed beverage begin its attack on the dozing occupant.

"That's not fair," came the cry.

"All's fair in war and coffee," Chris stated, paraphrasing a well-worn phrase.

"All right," she acknowledged as her disheveled head appeared from under the covers pulled up to her neck. "Let me get my nightgown."

She bent over the side of the bed and picked up the gown, growling as she noticed the rips in it. "Look at this. What happened to it?"

"I wonder," said Chris, chuckling a little. "Looks like it lost a battle," he said as he grabbed the bathrobe off the hook and handed it to her. "Here, use this, it doesn't rip as easily," he jokingly replied.

She stumbled out of bed, put on the robe and gingerly walked over to the couch and the breakfast tray, grabbing the hot cup of coffee before sitting down. "Where did this come from?" staring at the breakfast cart which resembled a miniaturized version of the breakfast downstairs.

"I had it sent up so we can relax and discuss the day's activities in private before joining society. Drink a little of your coffee first, and we can discuss it after," as he reached for a strawberry filled pastry. They sat quietly and let the morning slowly enter their bodies, awaken their senses, and come to life.

After the caffeine from the coffee and the sugar from the crème puff had made their appointed rounds through the tiny crevices that make up the human mind, Natalie turned to Chris and said, "I have a question."

"Oh God," he thought. "Here comes the morning-after question. I don't really know what to say, how to react. Should I just make light of it, or should I just let the heart talk and wait for the response? Either way I am bound to be wrong. I mean, a man can't talk about things like that. We aren't made like that. We can act, we can react, we can do all those types of things, but we can't talk about it the morning after. I mean, what do you say, 'well baby you could have been a little more active rather than just lying there' or 'the tongue action was a little lacking.'" Gathering up his strength he responded, "What is it?"

"Well," said Natalie, "I was wondering what you wanted to do today."

A huge sigh of relief escaped from Chris as he turned away.

"What was that," asked Natalie.

"Nothing," said Chris. "I was just coughing."

"Good," said Natalie, with the knowledge that God gave women the ability to know what a man is thinking without him even knowing what was on his own mind. It was a generic thing.

"I don't know, what about you?" questioned Chris, hoping to change the unspoken subject.

Natalie thought for a minute, then said, "Well, there are two things I thought about. I have always wanted to visit Switzerland and we are only a couple of hours away. Probably a little more as I would like to get to the heart of Switzerland, not just on the border. I heard a lot about a village at the end of the road, so to speak, right up against the Alps, called Lauterbrunnen. You can't go any further, at least by car. However, the brochure talked about a cog-train ride from there up to the Three Sisters, a little stop called Kleine Scheidegg known for its ski slopes and from there to Grindelwald and back to Lauterbrunnen. It's an all-day ride, but apparently worth it."

"Sounds nice, a little chilly perhaps, but nothing that warm soup won't cure," said Chris.

"The second idea," said Natalie, "was to travel north through the middle Rhine area to see two things. First the beautiful Cologne cathedral and learn some of its history, but perhaps more important, the American National Cemetery in Luxembourg which is the burial site of the soldiers lost during the Battle of the Bulge. Patton is buried there also, among his men. I would like to visit that and pay my respects. What do you think?"

Chris thought for a minute. "I would prefer going north and visiting the two places you mentioned. Especially the cemetery, but you know, let's talk to Theo when we check out and see what he has to say. But before we leave, we must do one thing."

"What would that be?"

"We saw the burning of the castle the other night, but we have not seen the inside of the castle. I would like to visit the castle, walk around the grounds, and get a feel for what life was like back when. I think it would be a fitting end to our stay here in Heidelberg."

"Good idea," said Natalie. "Let me finish this cup of coffee, take a shower, and change and we can get going. Shouldn't take too long."

"Sounds like a plan," said Chris, relieved that he had dodged The Question.

Chapter Twenty-Nine

"Good morning, Theo," said Chris as he and Natalie walked into the hotel office, each smiling to begin the day, the coffee having served its purpose.

"Morning," responded Theo as he stood up and extended his hand. "I hope you had a pleasant stay at our hotel."

"Absolutely," Natalie replied. "The room was exceptional, but more important, the service and attention to detail was superb. Your staff is to be congratulated!

"Great," smiled Theo. "So where are you off to today?"

"Well, we're not quite sure, but we have a few questions before we decide," said Natalie.

"Yes," said Chris. "We have had a wonderful time here in Heidelberg, seen a lot of things, met some wonderful people, not only from here, but from various places around the world visiting here. One thing we haven't done, which we wanted to do, is visit the beautiful castle above the city. Despite our map search, we see no roads leading there. How does one get to the castle?"

Theo laughed. "Yes, it is kind of hidden. You know the parking garage beyond the main plaza, perhaps you parked there?"

"I do," said Chris.

"Well, there is a small funicular in the building that takes you there." Before Chris could interject, Theo continued, "I know, it says 'Konigstuhl' indicating the top of the mountain. However, it stops halfway up and that is where you get off. From there, it is about thirty meters to the castle gate. A short walk. Buy the tickets at the kiosk, walk in, and enjoy yourself. Oh, and make sure you check out both the enormous balcony overlooking the city as well as the giant wine keg in the basement, large enough to hold a dance floor. You'll enjoy it."

"Thanks, Theo," said Natalie. "Now question number two. We are undecided on where to go next. I have always wanted to visit Switzerland, which is not far from here, couple of hours. But I have also always wanted to see the Middle Rhine with its numerous castles and churches, especially the Koln cathedral. What are your thoughts on that?"

Theo thought for a minute. "You know, there is a difference between visiting somewhere and getting to know somewhere. Reminds me of the movie 'If it's Tuesday, this must be Belgium.' If you spend an hour someplace, or even a day as a lot of the tourists' groups you see walking through our city following their guide with the raised colored flags so they don't get lost, they have visited Heidelberg. Unlike you who stayed here a couple of days walking around, eating in local places, chatting with people, and even sitting at Vetters watching the world go by. You know Heidelberg. So maybe the question 'do you want to know Germany, or do you want to visit other countries?' As for me, I would like to know rather than visit. But that is up to you."

Natalie looked at Chris for a moment, looking for some sign of his thoughts. He smiled and said, "I have always wanted to see the Koln cathedral since I was a little boy."

Natalie nodded. "Well," she said, "that was easy. Looks like we are headed north to the Rhine."

Theo smiled and nodded in acceptance of their decision.

"One final question, Theo. What is the tab for our wonderful stay?"

Theo looked into his desk drawer and pulled out a piece of paper with nothing written on it. "Here you go," he said and handed it to Chris.

Chris took the paper and looked at it. With a puzzled look on his face, he said, "This is blank. There is nothing on it."

"Yep," said Theo. "There is no charge."

"That's not right, Theo. You are running a business here. There must be something."

"Well, actually there is, but it has been taken care of."

"By whom?" asked Natalie.

"I was not supposed to say, it was to be a surprise, but your associate, Dieter, told me to put the tab on his bill and he'd take care of it. He said something about knowing his boss and his expense account would be approved."

Both Natalie and Chris shook their heads. "I'll take care of it," said Natalie.

Theo responded with a slight grin, "Dieter said you would."

With a final farewell, the couple headed to the castle to experience what it would be like to have been royalty during the castle's heyday. Two hours later, after spending time on the wide-open balcony overlooking the Old City with the Old Bridge and sipping a glass of wine while watching visitors clamor over the giant wine keg, they settled in the car and started their adventure north, to the Middle Rhine and the romance that goes with it.

An hour north of Heidelberg they exited the Autobahn and followed Highway 9, toward Bingen, Bacharach, Koblenz, and eventually Cologne. The kilometer markings kept getting lower and lower as the road followed the western side of the river, slowing every couple of kilometers to accommodate little towns and villages along the way, towns and villages which once belonged to the royalty that lived in the majestic castles hovering above them like guardians of their flock. It was a beautiful drive.

As the next sign appeared, it revealed the closeness with which all the countries of the region shared. The arrow pointing straight ahead said Bacharach. A second arrow pointed to the left and indicated "Luxembourg." Sitting up quickly, Natalie blurted out, "Turn left, turn now."

Chris looked bewildered. He was enjoying the ride and looking forward to getting to know more of Germany and now he was being asked to go to Luxembourg. What for?

"Why," he asked. "Why are we going to Luxembourg?"

"There is something I want us to see. It is important to me. Please turn."

Chris slowed the car down and made a left turn at the intersection. The sign read "Luxembourg 30 Kilometers."

"OK, I give. What is so important that our trip is interrupted?"

Natalie looked at him with a somber expression.

"The Luxembourg American Cemetery and Memorial," she said intently.

Chapter Thirty

The car pulled into the almost-empty parking lot, joining perhaps one or two other vehicles scattered on the black asphalt. Chris and Natalie slowly and reverently got out of their vehicle and stood silently staring at the huge iron gate anchored on each end by large stone pillars, both topped with a golden eagle as though beckoning visitors to enter and pay their respects.

They slowly walked through the gates and entered the building on the left, a sort of visitors' center explaining the memorial. A US Park Ranger greeted them as they entered and said, "Welcome to a little bit of America." Chris and Natalie looked at each other, questioning what they heard.

The Park Ranger giggled a little. "Yes, you heard me correctly. This is part of the United States. It was given to us by the government of Luxembourg in thanks for our liberation of their country during WW II, first, and second, so that American soldiers can be interred on American soil. It was a wonderful gesture, and quite honestly, gave me a job for which I am incredibly grateful."

The visitors' center was not large. It contained several pictures of the Memorial's construction, before and after shots, a podium for signing a visitors' book, a sand layout of the facility, and a few quotes from notable dignitaries from the United States. It was a quick visit and they soon left and walked to the main part of the Memorial.

As they passed the towering trees on their left, the sight of the over 5.000 graves came into view, each indicated by a white cross or Star of David. The grave markers were lined up as if in formation, long rows and columns of marble on both sides of a wide walkway separating the two sections of the cemetery.

White granite steps led down to the walkway and two water ponds with bellowing fountains added the only sound to the otherwise quiet scene. Only the beauty, the serenity, the peacefulness of the green grass punctuated by the white marble markers kept the sorrow and sadness of the grotesque memories of the fallen escaping from hell and ruining the dignity which lay before them.

Natalie sat down on the granite steps, looking slowly at the final resting places of the fallen soldiers.

"I hate war," she spoke quietly. "I hate it. It's such a waste of human life. I mean, look at this. 5000 people gone, like branches cut from a tree, a family tree. But not only are the branches cut and dead, but so are the new limbs that would have come from them, the new leaves, the birds sitting and singing, the butterflies, and the wonderful sounds the wind would make whistling its way through them. All gone.

Chris moved toward her and sat down on the steps alongside. His elbows rested on his knees and his head bowed as if in prayer. Occasionally his head would nod as if listening to someone speaking. Otherwise, he sat still, only hearing her voice and the sound of the water splashing into the pools.

"You know, perhaps we have this all wrong. Perhaps we are missing the whole thing. We talk about living and dying, like they are two separate things. But maybe they are not, and perhaps we have them reversed. Perhaps the time we spend on this earth, this moment in time eternal, is not life. Perhaps it is pre-life, a preparation for the true life which lies ahead. Perhaps it's just a period to get ready for what lies ahead.

"You see those fountains? Almost every cemetery you go to, there is a fountain. And that is because we believe water is the source of life. Without it nothing could live. But it is not the symbol of life here on earth, it is the symbol of life ahead. The fountains and the water splashing are not glorifying our time here, but rather celebrating our new life, like the ringing of the bells in church towers after the christening of a new child. The fountains are our bells, our celebration into a new life.

"I remember reading about funerals in the old south where the minstrels would play sobering music while pallbearers carried the casket to the cemetery followed by the family all dressed in black. Yet, after the burial, the music would be played loud and joyfully, with the family now dancing in the street in celebration of a new life for the deceased. Perhaps they had it right and we don't.

"So maybe when we mourn after the death of a loved-one, we mourn for ourselves, not for them. Maybe we just do not understand."

They sat there in silence, joining the over 5000 who have been silent for years. Natalie was thinking about the connection between war and death, between war and life, and between life and death. Chris sat there staring straight ahead, as though reliving a period of his life and wondering what is next.

"Chris," asked Natalie. "Have you ever been in a war."

Chris, without raising his head, murmured, "Yes."

"Yes?" said Natalie, in a questioning voice as if not expecting the answer.

"Yes."

There was a little pause. "What war, where?"

"Viet Nam," came the response.

"You were in Vietnam?" Chris nodded silently, looking straight down. "What did you do?"

"Infantry," came the response.

"No, I meant what did you do, what job did you have over there?"

"Infantry."

"No," said Natalie. "I mean what kind of work did you do in Viet Nam?"

Chris raised his head slowly, realizing that she had no idea what she was asking, just absolutely no idea.

With a raised head and a solid voice Chris turned to face Natalie and replied, "Kill."

The word lingered in the air, like a hot-air balloon only made of lead, an unlikely candidate for a sober moment such as this.

"My job was to kill the enemy, and to do so before he killed me."

Stunned is too mild of a word for the emotions that Natalie felt. Waves of questions overflowed her mind, none with answers. She wanted to know it all, to know how it felt, to know the level of fear, of fright, of anguish, of pain, and surely prayer that a soldier felt in that situation.

What did it feel like? What did you do? How did you handle it? What did you feel when a friend got injured or even killed? How did it affect your mind, your psyche, your desire to not be there? How, how, how. Tell me but don't tell me. I want to know but keep quiet. I want to understand but don't explain. I want, I want, I want. I don't want.

"Chris," she quietly said. "I'm sorry," and reached over to put her hand in his.

He put his second hand over hers and slowly nodded. "Me too."

And he started to talk. He talked about the training he got before going to Viet Nam. How it turned out to be useless because the jungle in Panama was nothing like the jungle in Viet Nam. The terrain was different, mountains versus rice paddies, trees versus sabre-sharp grasses, and the people, the Vietnamese, sometimes your friend during the day, and then hoping to kill you are night. It was one terrible nightmare that lasted 365 days. One year. The longest year he could remember.

Natalie stared at him. This was a part of him she did not know, did not expect, and didn't know how to react. She sat there waiting for him to continue speaking. He didn't. And she felt empty, unfulfilled, and honestly, a little ashamed, a little ashamed at herself because she had let heart run ahead of her head.

But, she rationalized, she was not at fault. The subject had not come up, and probably would not have come up had she not wanted to visit the Memorial. She was not at fault, just as he was not at fault. He had sworn an oath, a duty, and had complied with that oath. He had kept his word. There is nothing to be ashamed about that.

Despite her desire to move on, two thoughts, two questions remained, like apples hanging from a tree just waiting to be harvested and reinvented as something else. She thought about asking them, first yes, then no, then yes again, like an endless ping-pong match with the answer shifting from one side to the other.

Chris raised his head and looked at the confused look on her face. In a moment of pity he said, "I know what you are thinking and it's a natural thing to ask but also an uncomfortable thing to ask. So let me relieve you of that problem. You want to know if I had any friends killed in Viet Nam."

He thought for a minute.

"You didn't have any friends in Viet Nam. Oh, you had acquaintances, you had buddies, you even had bunker-mates. But you did not have friends. You see, friends denote a special relationship, a relationship that spans over time; a relationship that talks to the future, that talks to gatherings in the back yard, to camping trips with one another, to kids' birthday, graduations, weddings, and grandkids. That's what friends are. But in a situation like war, there is no guarantee that future would occur for in a few fleeting seconds all those happy occasions could be lying next to you, gasping for breath and crying for their Momma. And, in all honestly, it would rip out your gut."

"So, you build a little wall around yourself, keeping civil but distant, keeping friendly but aloof, keeping concerned but professional, keeping alert and aware. So, to answer your unasked question, while I had buddies that would no longer be among the living, no, I did not have any friends die in Viet Nam."

He looked at her as she stared at him. Every word he said seemed to sink deeply into her being bringing an enlightenment that rarely came to be. She appreciated his openness, his willing to speak of such things, and respected his decision to dig into the past to try and answer her questions. Few people had done so and he was relieved to respond without the fear of recriminations.

"And I know there is one more question you want answered but are too afraid to ask. Well, let me relieve you of that burden. As far as I know, I did not kill anyone. But let's be honest. It was not because I didn't try but in a jungle war, you just don't know. You hear rifle shots, you hear screams, you see muzzle flashes, but you don't see people. And so, you respond, you respond to an area from which all the action came. You fire at a bush, a tree, a hutch. You empty your clip, slam another one in, and fire some more. And you keep at it until there are no more shots, no more flashes, nothing but silence. Did you kill anyone? You don't know. And when you went to investigate the area, there was nothing there as the enemy was careful in carrying away their dead. So you don't know. And I don't know."

"Chris, I am so sorry to have made you recall a painful time in your life, both physical and mentally. I am so sorry. But I can tell you one thing, I have never jumped so high in my life."

"It's getting late, we better go. I'll drive."

Chapter Thirty-One

The stench of war long remains after the last shot is fired. It follows one around like a tiger on a leash waiting to pounce at the least provocation. And yesterday, at the Cemetery, it pounced on Chris. and despite the re-caging of the beast, it lurked around for the remainder of the evening and into the morning.

The ride to Oberwesel and the hotel recommended by Trio, Weinhaus Weiler, was noticeably quiet. Each of them immersed in their own thoughts and ideas, and each hoping and silently pleading for the other to return to reality. But it was not to be, and the evening ended with a gracious hug and kiss and the roaring of the train outside the open window. Neither of which lasted long.

The following morning, after the usual rituals, Chris and Natalie walked downstairs to the impeccably dressed dining room and sat at the table designated by a silver card holder with their names delicately written on it. Chris laughed as he sat down. Natalie stared at the crack in the façade and wondered.

"What are you laughing at?" she asked.

Chris looked at her and smiled. "I was just checking the name cards at the other tables. Each had a nametag with the last name on it. Ours, on the other hand, said, 'Natalie and Chris.' Guess they couldn't decide which last name to use," he said, chuckling again.

Natalie laughed along with him and said, "Nice to hear you laugh again. I missed it."

Chris looked her straight in the eye. "Me too," he said. "Now, let's eat, I'm famished!"

Halfway through their breakfast, Trude, the wife and co-owner of the Gasthaus, came over to check on them. "How are you doing this morning? Is the food enough for you?"

Both Chris and Natalie nodded in the affirmative, trying to finish their mouthfuls before talking. Natalie responded first. "The food is wonderful, and this room is beautiful. Did someone decorate it for you?"

"No," laughed Trude. "My daughter and I threw it together one afternoon and it has stayed that way for several years. We threaten to change it every couple of years but Klaus, my husband, wouldn't allow it. He says why change perfect. Guess he is right."

"Perfect is right," said Natalie. "And speaking of perfect, that goulash soup you fixed for us was outstanding. Thank you."

"You're welcome! So, what are your plans for the day? Looks like a nice sunny day. Good for being outdoors."

"Well," said Natalie, "we were planning on driving up along the river to Koblenz. Like you said, it is a beautiful day, and the drive should be nice."

Trude looked at her watch and responded, "A suggestion if you don't mind. In about forty-five minutes a river cruiser will stop at the dock in the park along the river heading to Koblenz. I suggest you take the trip. It is quiet, comfortable, and a bit slower than the car, giving more time to enjoy the view. It takes about two hours to Koblenz. Have lunch there and take the train back here in time for dinner. An enjoyable day trip, relaxing and serene. Just a suggestion, though."

Thirty minutes later Natalie and Chris had crossed under the town's old wall and were walking through the park to the simple dock up ahead. They could see the cruiser making its way down the river to the dock and fifteen minutes later they had stepped board the ship, climbed the stairs to the top deck and settled at a table along the outer rail, offering an amazing view of the surrounding area and the views to come. A couple of cups of Capuchino sealed the deal and they sighed and watched as the cruiser resumed its daily trip down-river to Koblenz before heading back to its home port.

Chris turned to Natalie, his elbows resting on the table and his hands clenched under his chin. "Why did you ask me those questions at the cemetery yesterday?"

Natalie looked at him, not sure how to answer. But it was too late, her hands did it for her. For they lay flat on the table, palms up as though saying, "I have nothing to hide. I have nothing to fear in letting you know me, my inner feelings are there for you to see, to examine, to criticize, or to caress and care for. It is your choice. I have made mine."

With a clear and confident voice, she responded, "The first question, were you in a war, was easy to ask. It was mandated by the environment in which we found ourselves. For before us were the reminders of war, barely covered with a thin veneer of green grass, punctuated with white crosses and the Stars of David. Lying beneath that veneer were the dreams and hopes of thousands of people whose lives were lost and whose families were torn by their sacrifice. It was an easy question. But the answer surprised me. I never thought you had experienced war. You lived in a nice neighborhood, had a good family, your parents were prosperous and respected, you became an Ivy League graduate you had, and have connections enabling you to be where you are today. Surely you could have gotten out of serving. A well-placed phone call was all it would have taken. Why?"

In a somber and even voice, Chris responded, "I volunteered."

A look of astonishment came over Natalie. And out of her mouth, echoing the same question asked by a multitude of mothers, finances', and girlfriends, and perhaps only understood by fathers who had also faced the same situation, the one question which digs at the very heart of every decision a person makes, the one word, three little letters leading to one big void, "Why?"

Chris chuckled a little as Natalie looked on with wonder. "It is amazing," he explained, "how often adding a single word to the premise proceeding a question, answers the same question, from a little different perspective. Take the world 'because.'

"Yes, because I came from a good neighborhood, because I had a good family, because my parents were well respected, and because they were well-off, because I was an Ivy League graduate, because I had friends in influential positions, and because they could have helped me if I had asked. It was all of these 'becauses' that I chose to make my own path. You see, there are 'takers' and 'givers' in this world. I could have easily fallen into the 'takers' fold, moved on to something else and let others handle the burden. Millions do. But millions do not or did not have the opportunities that I did. So, I like to think I did the right thing.

"But don't misunderstand me. I did not stand alone. There were millions who chose the same path and while most of them came home, some with pieces missing, some with dark memories that will last forever. And some laying in metal coffins, having chosen the same path as me, but with different results. But they all, in their own minds, chose their right path. I am proud to be among them.

"And that, my dear, is 'why.'"

Chapter Thirty-Two

A silence filled the boat even as music blared from the horn-shaped speakers and children ran around the metal deck to see which could reach the goal first. Parents joyfully laughed as the kids played, sipping their wine and cold beer while pretending to watch beautiful sights of castles and vineyards roll past like clouds in the windy sky.

Yet, silence prevailed.

Between the two of them, there was no noise. Whatever noise there had been was reduced to a whimper, something so far off into the distance that it was of no matter.

What was of matter was the connection between two people that neither had intended, nor even knew they desired: a connection that had grown as natural as leaves on a tree in the spring, as grass on the ground, and more importantly, as flowers blooming with the joy of having lived through the rigors of winter at the sight of the warmth of the sun and the taste of summer. If that were life, it would be good. If not, it should be.

With two hands joined together, they watched as hundreds of years of history opened their arms to the gazing travelers. It was a wonderful trip, made even more wonderful by their own discovery, their own history in the making. All was right with the world.

The ship moved effortlessly toward the dock, its crew ready and willing to jump to the pier and snuggle their vessel tightly and safely to its temporary home.

Kids, once eager to be the first to reach the goal, were now challenging each other to be the first off the ship, their parents struggling to keep up with them and make sure they stayed dry. Natalie and Chris waited their turn, then silently made their way to dry land. The captain of the ship stood by and Chris shook his hand and thanked him for a wonderful trip down the river. The captain nodded and smiled, for that is what they paid him to do.

The walk to the Deutches Ecke was a quick stroll of three blocks, all along the bank of the river and affording a serene view of the cable car stretching above the river to the huge fortress atop the high hills overlooking the confluence of the Rhine and the Moselle, comprising the Deutches Ecke or German Corner.

It is here that the mighty Rhine merges with the graceful and elegant Moselle to continue its march to the North Sea. It is here that the bronze statue of Bismark rises above the park celebrating the unification of the Germanic tribes into one nation, at least until the end of WW II when the country was split in two. It is here that Natalie and Chris moved as one, reflecting the spiritual unification of the scene, otherwise obscured in the beauty of the moment. And it is here they found the ice cream shop.

For some reason, vanilla ice cream with chocolate sauce speared by a sugar cookie puts everything into perspective. At least it seems that way.

Chris looked at Natalie across the table topped with a checkered table-cloth and said, "So, you have learned a little about my inner self the past few days, which I was happy to share, but it's payback time. Now you. What is it bout this little girl, you know, the one who heads up a large international shipping airline, the one who controls the fate of so many people, and who, by the way, is admired by both her employees and her competitors, what is it a man like me, someone in this position, which I have yet to figure out and much less. understand, should know? Please tell!! Oh, and don't bother about all the business stuff. I've read your resume, impressive but dull. I want the real stuff. What makes Natalie, Natalie?"

Natalie looked amused and chuckled. "I really don't know what to tell you," Natile said in a quiet voice. "You know the story about my mom and her father leaving this country and moving to America to avoid another world conflict. She was pregnant during the move but did not know it. My father, a pilot, disappeared during the Berlin Blockade and my mother never saw him again till that fateful day. Meanwhile, I was born in this tiny Midwest town inhabited by mostly German immigrants and grew up with a lot of the German customs and traditions, and more importantly, it's values. It was a good life, not without its challenges, but a good life.

"After high school I was faced with the prospect of staying home and settling down or doing something else. It was literally a conflict of values, on the one hand the idea of staying with family and building a life which closely includes them, and on the other hand, the typical German value of working hard to make oneself better. In my particular case, they were mutually exclusive. The town, and area itself, had no opportunity for that betterment. It provided the family traditions and closeness, but left one without a chance of self-fulfillment. The idea of doing something different won out, and I applied for, and received a scholarship for the New Jersey college. Why New Jersey you asked? Because of its proximity to New York, the big stage, the Big Apple, and the chance of landing there. Mom was not pleased, but understood and accepted it.

"College was a challenge. I was different. Most of the girls were from New Jersey, knew each other from other circles, and quickly formed cliques. I was not in any of them and felt left out. So, I concentrated on my studies and did well."

"Wait," said Chris with a questioning look. "You never had any social interaction, either with the other girls or the guys in the school across town?"

"Oh, there were a few concerts or lawn parties that I attended, oh, and some football games, especially against Princeton. You've heard of that school, haven't you?" she asked the Princeton graduate.

Chris grinned. "Yea, I was one of the gate guards searching people for stuff they weren't allowed to bring into the stadium, you know, like alcohol, things like that. In fact, never did understand while students from your school always showed up with bags of oranges, supposedly to eat rather than buying the expensive food at the vendors. Still puzzles me."

Natalie laughed.

"What are you laughing at?" asked Chris.

"You don't know, even now?"

She smiled. "We spent all Saturday mornings injecting those oranges with vodka using syringes. They were full of alcohol. We would pour the vodka into bowls at the fraternity house, load the syringes up with the vodka and inject the oranges. One or two pokes and it was done. Throw it into a bag and on to the next one. Didn't you ever wonder why we were happy leaving, even after we lost? Who cared?"

Chris stared back in wonder. He shook his head side to side. "And I stood outside looking at all those cheap bastards. They had it better than me. I may have gone to the wrong school!"

Natalie chuckled as she looked at her watch, the shadows growing longer. "We had better get to the train station. It's getting late and we don't want to miss our reservations at the castle. I'm looking forward to that!"

"What, you don't want another orange?" Chris quizzed.

Natalie starred back. "No, I like my wine."

"Same thing," said Chris, "just a different fruit."

"I'm likin' this," thought Natalie as they grabbed a cab to the station and headed back to Oberwesel and dinner at the castle.

Chapter Thirty-Three

The hostess led them through several stone rooms dominated by huge fireplaces till they emerged onto the outside patio nestled against the walls of the keep and protected by the ramparts on the other side. Their table was snug against the outside wall, covered with a white tablecloth and adorned with a copper plate on which sat an unlit candle surrounded by greenery from the local forest.

Natalie and Chris sat down as the hostess told them the waiter would be right with them. Curious, they both looked out over the rampart at the small town, its early evening lights beginning to appear and the mighty river flowing beside it, unceasingly to its destination. It was as it had been for hundreds of years.

A young waiter approached their table with a cheerful smile and a bright hello, she said, "Welcome to Castle Schonburg. I hope thing are going well for you today."

The couple looked up as Natalie replied, "Very well, thank you and hope yours as well."

"It is," responded the waiter as he reached behind himself to his assistant who stood with a silver tray holding two glasses of wine. The waiter gently caressed the wine glasses and settled them on the table, the red wine before Natalie and the white wine in front of Chris.

Chris looked confused and said, "I don't remember ordering wine. Where did these come from?"

The waiter smiled. "Well, they actually come from the local winery, part of the castle grounds, but were ordered by Frau Weiler, Trudel, who knew what you liked and asked that we provide them to you, with her compliments. Hope you enjoy!"

"I am sure we shall," said Chris. "Oh, by the way, we are ready to order."

Surprised, the waiter said, "But you haven't even seen the menu yet."

"Ah," said Chris, "but we have. Apparently, you have given a copy of the menu to the local gasthauses to entice guests to your restaurant. We checked it out at Weinhaus Weiler before coming here, so we are ready to order."

"Very good, Sir, and what can I get you?"

Chris looked over at Natalie and smiled. "With all due respect to your German cuisine, we are a little tired of schnitzel and corden bleu or rolladen, so something a little different tonight. We would like to try the chateaubriand for two, please."

The waiter looked up, quite surprised. "Excellent choice, Sir. That is our chef's favorite meal to cook. I am sure you know, but that will take a little extra time to get it exactly right, if that is OK?"

"Quite," said Chris. Looking over at Natalie, he said, "We have a lot to talk about."

The waiter nodded slightly, turned, and walked away. Chris leaned forward and said, "OK, so where were we?"

Natalie looked a little surprised. "Where were we?" she asked. "Not sure what you mean?"

"Well, you were telling me about how you got to where you are. I think we left off with drunken oranges. But it's a long way from drunken oranges to the CEO of a major airline. There has to be something in between that I need to know about."

Natalie laughed. "Yea, drunken oranges to airline CEO in one easy step. Sounds like a 'How To' book," as she chuckled. Resting her chin in her hands, she glanced once more at the wonderful sight below her and allowed herself to open up and began to speak.

"As graduation approached, I did the normal things a graduating senior would do, which included looking for a job. While in college, we all had a career in mind and longed for that opportunity. But as graduation came closer and closer, career search transformed into a job search. While I always had the option of returning home, that is not what I wanted. Oh, I loved my mother, my grandfather, and the community in which I was raised, but it was not for me, especially after spending four years in an urban environment. I wanted something else.

"Well, nothing else came along. Not sure why. Tried to figure it out so I could fix it but not successful. I finally rationalized that it was because I was an outsider, not an East Coaster, not a New Englander, not a New Yorker. I was an unknown quality, and therefore didn't fit. I don't know if that was true, but I told myself it was and that I somehow had to adjust to fit in. I just didn't know how.

"As graduation approached, nothing appeared until one morning my career counselor showed me an ad for an intern position at a medical products company right in town. I knew nothing about medical products, nor cared to learn about them, but the opportunity seemed to be the only one available. So, I took it. It was the biggest mistake, and the greatest learning experience, I had even made. I thank the powers that be that I did."

"Sounds like somewhat of a dichotomy," said Chris. "Mistake and learning experience, all in one shot. That had to be something."

"Yes," said Natalie. "While the program was an innovative idea, its implementation was terrible. In the six months of the program, I was introduced to about ten different departments. I spent about two to three weeks in each one, learned little, produced little, and impressed hiring managers even less. It was not an environment within which to display one's talents or abilities. In essence, you sat at a desk, one of many, all in a row, like grammar school, with the manager or supervisor at the front like a headmaster. There was no interaction, there was no personality, there was no comradeship, there was nothing. One could not even have pictures of family or loved ones on the desk. They were for work only. And the phones, eh, if they didn't ring, don't touch them. If somebody wanted to talk with you, they would call you, you didn't need to call anyone. That was what the manager was for. So, when it came time to be offered a full-time position, my name was not selected. And am I glad now. Not then, as I was back to square one, but in reality, it was the best thing."

The waiter approached them. He said, "Excuse me, but the chef asked me to advise you that your dinner will be served in about ten minutes in case you needed to wash up or use the facilities. As the meal is best served hot, it is well you are not interrupted while dining."

"Thank you," said Chris. Looking at Natalie he said, "Please continue."

And so, she did. Continuing, Natalie said, "Just a couple of days before my last day at the medical company I was looking through the Newark paper and found a small ad looking for an assistant with proposal preparation experience. I had a little of that, very little, so, as most desperate people do, I exaggerated a little on the cover letter and a few days later was asked to come in for an interview. It turned out the company was Condor Airlines located at Newark Airport.

"I got there a couple of minutes early, met with someone from HR and waited for the interview. A little while later, a young woman led me upstairs to what looked like an anteroom or lobby, with a single desk stationed like a guard before a door leading to what appeared to be a large office with lots of windows. An older woman was seated at the desk, looked up and motioned for me to sit opposite her and the younger woman left us alone.

'Hello,' said the older woman. 'You are here for the proposal preparation job, right?'

'Yes Ma'am,' I said.

'Well, tell me a little about yourself?'

"I proceeded to give my one-minute sales pitch, emphasizing my proposal experience with the medical company, and told her how excited I was to be able to help them. It seemed to be going well, with a little back and forth. Suddenly, a man appeared in the office door and asked the woman to join him in the office and close the door behind her. So, I was left there alone.

"As I sat there in front of the desk, the phone on the desk began to ring. It stopped and a minute later, it rang again. This was going on non-stop for what I thought was an eternity. Finally, a little exasperated, I walked around the desk and began answering the phone, pretending to be an assistant. I took notes, directed callers to others to answer their questions, and basically operated as an answering machine. A copy of minutes later, the older woman exited the office, stopped short of her desk, and asked me what I was doing.

'What are you doing,' the woman asked, who I later learned was named Margaret.

'I was answering your phone, it just seemed that if people were calling you, it was something important and should be addressed right away. I took a lot of notes for you on who called and their reasons and forwarded some calls to what I thought were the right offices. I meant no hard, just trying to help.'

"The woman looked at me, motioned me to take my original seat and poured through the notes I had taken. She had a few questions which I tried to answer about the calls and that was it. To my surprise, she picked up the phone, put it on speaker, and spoke to the other end. I remember her saying 'Janet, please suspend the ad in the paper and cancel any other interviews. I believe I have found the person I want.'

"And that," said Natalie, "is how I ended up at Condor. The rest you know from reading the papers and news articles after Ron, my father, died. As a result, I became CEO and Chairperson of the Board. How's that for a 'How To' story?"

The waiter wheeled a glass-covered cart over to the table, a polished silver top covered the chateaubriand, vegetables, and potatoes. With a show of expertise, he sliced the meat into thin medallions, arranged them on delft dishes and placed the meals before Chris and Natalie.

"Please enjoy and let me know if there is anything else I can do or get for you. Bon Appetit!"

Chris looked at Natalie. "You look famished. Let's eat."

The receptionist held open the massive wooden door as the sated couple carefully negotiated the steps to the lower courtyard. Walking gingerly on the cobblestones, they quickly came to the flat drawbridge and the waiting parking lot.

Natalie slipped into the front seat as Chris held the door, then walked to the driver's side and slid into his seat. He tentatively placed both hands on the steering wheel and stared straight ahead as though in a trance. Natalie turned and looked at him.

"Are you all right?" she asked with a worried look on her face.

"I'm fine," he whispered. "It's just that this evening was a wonderful event for me, not necessarily for the food, but for the fact that you opened up to me, explained to me your thinking, your desires, your actions. Something a news clipping or article could never do. And I do appreciate it. You have made me a happy man. And is there nothing more important to a man than finding a woman who makes him happy? I thank you."

Natalie listened and listened some more. Behind the words there was much more and she began to see it. She reached over and placed her hand on his as if to say, "you're welcome." Though the words were not spoken, they were conveyed willingly and openly.

"I had better get us back to the hotel before the water in my eyes ruins my vision," said Chris as he started the car.

"Me too," spoke Natalie quietly. "Please go."

Chris drove the car the longest short route to the hotel. With no hesitation, they entered the Gasthaus, climbed the stairs to their room, and closed the door behind them, leaving the rest of the world behind.

Chapter Thirty-Four

The sleek black magic carpet with the Mercedes emblem on its front whisked the couple through the gated city wall and into the realm of reality, away from the mythical and enchanted vision of medieval Germany and back into the urbanization of the modern world.

An hour and a half later the magic carpet pulled into the visitor's parking spot in front of Condor headquarters at the Frankfurt International Airport and Chris and Natalie exited and walked into the front lobby.

The receptionist, having already seen them pull in, alerted Dieter of their arrival and he joyfully greeted them as they entered.

"Welcome back," he said. "How was your short tour?"

"It was great, Dieter, thanks for asking. Oh, and thanks for your hospitality in Heidelberg. We enjoyed meeting Theo, and the room was fantastic, but there was no need for taking care of the bill at the hotel. We could have handled it."

"I'm sure you could," said Dieter with a smile. "But Theo and I are old friends and he owed me a favor, so no harm, no foul as they say in that stupid game, whatever it is. Come into my office and we can discuss your plans for the rest of your time here."

With that the three of them scooted down the hall to Dieter's office and settled round the conference table. "So, what is next on the agenda?" asked Dieter.

"Well," replied Natalie, "we both have some catching up to do back home so the use of a couple of offices would be welcomed, with international phone service if possible. Then back to the hotel and rest up for the little party we have tomorrow in Oberstdorf with my mother's friends from the village. Then back to the States the next day, so," she hesitated, "we may not see you again before we leave."

"Ah yes, I was thinking about that and figured out a way to assist in your party going. I will have one of my people drive you to

Oberstdorf, wait for you, and drive you back to the hotel."

"Dieter, there is no reason for that. We know how to get there."

"Understand, but you are going to a party, and, as at all parties, there will be drinks, beer, wine, a little schnapps, who knows. I want you to have an enjoyable time and not worry about driving back, and besides, you won't have to worry about dropping the car back here. You can take the hotel shuttle to the terminal in the morning without the hassle. It works well."

"Sounds like a plan. We appreciate that. Now, we will get out of your hair if you show us the offices. We'll stop by before leaving to say goodbye."

"OK," said Dieter. "Follow me."

Hours later the car left the hotel leaving Natalie and Chris walking to the receptionist.

The receptionist, recognizing them, said, "Welcome Ms. Matthews and Mr. Palermo, welcome back. I have your rooms ready. They are both on the 5th floor, just a couple of doors down from each other."

"Oh," said Chris. "I forgot to ask for adjoining rooms. We are going to be working together this evening, in fact going to order dinner from room service and we would like adjoining rooms if possible."

The receptionist smiled and asked, "Do you mean adjoining, or connecting rooms?"

"Actually, connecting rooms would be better so we can use both phones at the same time. Connecting will be fine," he said.

The receptionist checked her list, flipped a couple of pages, and smiled. "Here we are," she said. "Seventh floor, connecting rooms, right near the elevator so not far of a walk. Is that all right with you?"

"Great," said Chris. "Thank you very much."

He and Natalie turned to walk away toward the elevators. As they left the receptionist desk a couple of steps behind, Natalie leaned slightly over to whisper in Chris' ear, "You cad!"

He turned to look at her, resumed his blank stare toward the elevator and returned her whisper. "You're welcome!"

The receptionist heard the whispered conversation and smiled knowingly.

Chapter Thirty-Five

The car pulled up to the Gasthaus and stopped in front of the door. Natalie and Chris got out, thanked the driver, and offered to have him come in and get something to eat.

"No thanks," said the driver. "I'll just park over here in this lot and wait for you. I have a couple of books to read. This new novel, 'The German Triangle' sounds interesting. I'll let you know how it is."

"Fine," said Natalie. "We'll be a couple of hours. Come in if you feel bored."

Chris opened the outer door for Natalie and the sound of voices escaped from the inside. Opening the inner door, Natalie saw the dining room of the Gasthaus zum Rose all decorated with balloons, streamers, and a huge welcome sign hanging over the bar. She smiled as she walked in.

Sigrid saw the door open and Natalie and Chris enter the room and immediately went over to greet them. She gave them both a warm hug and called Tomas and Sophie, who both came out of the kitchen to welcome them. With a little fanfare she ushered them to the Stammtisch, the family table, and when Natalie turned and looked surprised, she said, "You are family. Please sit."

Natalie looked around the room and saw several tables already occupied by people, mostly elderly people who knew Sigrid by name. Wine glasses and beer mugs adorned the tables and more sat on the bar obviously waiting to be used. Several more people entered the room and were heartly greeted by those already there. As more and more people arrived, the noise level increased until finally Sigrid got up and stood in front of the bar.

"Hello dear friends. Thank you for coming today as it is a special day for us all," she said in German. Realizing that neither Natalie nor Chris spoke German, she motioned Sophie to translate into English what she said and was going to say. Sophie moved to stand beside grandmother, happy to be of assistance. "Those of us here remember my cousin, Ingrid, who moved to the United States to escape the war. She had a daughter whom we never met, until today. Today she is visiting us and bringing back old memories," pointing to Natalie. A slight murmur and applause sprang from the tables as they all looked over at Natalie. She waved and bowed in acknowledgment with a huge grin.

Sigrid moved over to Natalie and took her hand and walked her over to each and every one of the guests. And with each one, Natalie heard stories after stories of her mother, her young life, her school dances and parties, her young loves, her trips to Paris and Madrid, and even to Italy with her class.

It was a part of her mother's life about which she knew nothing and it astonished her to learn of all the things that her mother had done. It was a journey she had not expected but welcomed with an open heart. It filled a void that had remained locked away, like a secret closet or hidden drawer.

A void that contained the elements, the foundation of what had made her mother. It was like the opening of a soul, the locked container holding the building blocks of a person, the intricate and intimate experiences that led to the person later in life. It was Ingrid as a child, as a teenager, as a young woman, as an adult. It completed the image, the person she loved and cared for, and like the final brush strokes on a masterpiece, it was signed with a final brush of the hair and a softly spoken "I love you."

Finally, it was time to go. Natalie had spent most of the afternoon meeting new friends and learning about her mother. Chris, on the other hand, sat at the table and watched, occasionally joined by John who, between stints in the kitchen, came over to sit with him and engage with him in some conversations before resuming his role as kitchen back-up to Tomas. They both enjoyed watching the scene before them, but both knew it was time to leave.

Natalie, through Sophie, thanked all for coming and for sharing their wonderful experiences with her mother. She hugged Sigrid and Sophie as well as Tomas and thanked them for arranging such an afternoon. With tears in her eyes, she left the little Gasthaus and walked to the waiting car. As the car pulled away, she leaned over and placed her head on Chris' chest, and wept. Never had she been so happy in all her life.

Chapter Thirty-Six

Chris was sitting in the over=stuffed chair reading a hotel magazine and watching Natalie pack her suitcase when the phone rang. Natalie looked at Chris, who starred, stretched out his arms with his palms up, shrugged his shoulders as if to say "I don't know."

She walked over to the phone, picked it up and answered "Hello?"

"Oh, hi. How are you doing today?"

"Just packing, getting ready to head back stateside."

"You what?"

"Now?"

"Can't this wait till we get home?"

"OK, give me five minutes and I'll be down."

Natalie turned to Chris. "That was John."

"I figured."

"You figured? Why?"

"He told me he would call."

"Told you? When?"

"Yesterday, at the party."

"Do you know what he wants to talk about?"

"Yep."

"Can you tell me?"

"Nope."

"Why not?"

"Made me promise."

"So, I am supposed to be surprised?"

"Sort of."

"So, I am supposed to go down there and not be prepared?"

"I guess so."

"So, you're not telling me?"

"Nope."

Natalie looked confused. And upset. Chris knew but he wouldn't say anything. She hastily finished dressing and walked to the door.

Turning, she said, "Last chance."

Chris responded with "Have a good chat," as he turned the page of the magazine. The door shut a little harder than usual. Chris chuckled.

The elevator door opened and Natalie walked out, looked around and spotted John sitting at a table in the lobby. She walked over and sat down across the table glaring at the young man.

"OK, John, what is so important that it can't wait till we get home?"

With a slight hesitation, John asked her how her day was yesterday.

"Super," she said. "A little sad, but it was a fun time and I got to learn a little about my mother that I did not know, or at least did not realize. I hope it was not too much work for them to host it. I know it was a lot. Germany is a wonderful country and I hope to come back some day."

"That is what I want to talk to you about," said John. He exhaled deeply. "I want to stay here a little longer."

Natalie leaned back in her chair and paused. "You still have more to learn from Dieter?" she asked. "How much more? And how much longer do you think you need? You know Dick would like you back as soon as possible."

John looked unimpressed with her questions. Frustrated, Natalie sat erect, looked John straight in the eyes and asked him the most important question.

"OK, John. Why?"

Why? Three little letters followed by an upside-down fishhook, an innocent looking word, but asking so much. It cuts right to the core of the matter, brushes away all the garbage in the path, and asks you to bare your soul, reveal your inner feelings, and expose the true meaning of what you said.

"Why, John?"

John leaned forward in his chair, clasped his hands together, and rested his elbows on the table between them. His head lowered till it stopped on the clasped hands. Raising his head, he returned the straight look, and started.

"A while back I heard a story about a young German woman who lived in a small village not too far from here. She lived alone with her father in the Gasthaus they owned because her mother had died a horrible death when the house in which she was cooking dinner was demolished by a German fight plane that had been shot down by the Allies. The young woman was devastated by the event and developed a hatred for anyone in uniform, regardless of which side, and especially anyone who was a pilot. So, while American pilots frequented the Gasthaus from the local airfield, she stayed aloof, went about her business, and refused to socialize with any of them.

"That was until a couple of left-over Hitler-youths came to the Gasthaus and started beating her crippled father because of his verbal distain for Nazis. He was no match for the young guys and was due to be severely beaten until one of young American pilots came to the rescue, and while the pilot sustained some minor physical damage, her father was saved from far worse.

"It was then, after an evening of reflection, that she realized that neither the uniform, nor the duties one had to perform, made the person. It was then that she realized that her disdain for this soldier, and many others, was misplaced and needed to be reexamined. So, she began to talk with the pilots, especially the one that had rescued her father. Over time, and many conversations, a relationship developed between her and this pilot, a relationship so strong that it fertilized intimacy between them and talk of spending their whole lives together.

"But alas, world events, which had brought them together, wrestled them apart. The Berlin Blockade began and the pilot was called to execute his duty. While all seemed to be going as well as expected, a crash of his airplane forced his evacuation to the States, losing contact with her, never to be recovered until the last days of their lives.

"But, as fate would have it, this woman was pregnant, and her father, for many reasons, decided to immigrate to the United States, to be far away from his fear of a third world war, but mostly to allow his daughter to grow up, give birth in a community which knew little of them, and get on with her life. And that happened. And while the woman waited and waited for her White Knight to reappear, it never happened and she lived a solitary life, with the exception of her father until he moved on, and her daughter, who moved East to begin her own saga."

John raised his head and with a voice bolstered and supported by a sense of conviction and righteous, and said, "I don't want that to happen to Sophie. You see, Natalie, I have become her White Knight."

The silence was deafening. No where, no how, had this been expected. It was totally out of the blue.

"John, it has only been a week since you met her."

"I know," said John. "And it has been wonderful. And to your thought, maybe it has not been long enough to make such a judgment. And maybe more time is needed. But the separation of the Atlantic Ocean is not going to allow that time to take place. What I am asking for is the time to find out. Next week, next month, who knows, we may realize that it is not to be. But, after the same time, we may know it is to be. I am asking for that time. I'll still work for Condor, work for Dieter, learn more about international trade and travel and become more valuable to our work. But I have to do this, with or without your permission."

Another hour went by and Chris began to worry when a knock came on the door. He opened and Natalie walked in like a zombie, her eyes focused on, on nothing, and her face marred with the bottled "natural look" stuff that women wear. It was not a pretty sight, and he worried.

"I said yes," said Natalie in a whimper.

"I knew you would."

"I hate you," she said as she rushed to hold on to the most secure thing in her life. And grasping Chris, her arms locked around his neck and forcing her head into his chest, she said with a loving whisper, "I hate you."

Chris chuckled to himself and thought, "You know, there is not much difference between hate and love. Both harbor the same intense feelings and while light may shine on the differences, take the light away and beneath it all, love hides. For the opposite of love is not hate, it is indifference. Indifference means you don't care, don't worry, don't think about. But not hate. Hate reflects the same thoughts and ideas as love, only like two trains heading in the opposite direction on an oval track. But when they join together at the bottom of the track, love and hate couple, merging together as one."

"That's a good start," he reasoned with a slightly larger smile as he held her tight.

Chapter Thirty-Seven

Eight hours is eight hours. It doesn't matter if you are in a warm and cozy bed in the dead of winter, eight hours is eight hours. Of if you are exceedingly productive in the office that day, eight hours is still eight hours. But step into that shiny metallic cigar-shaped machine churning away at 500 to 600 hundred miles per hour at 30 to 40 thousand feet above the earth, and eight hours is not eight hours.

Eight hours is an eternity. And whether you are enjoying the amenities of First Class, thanks to Dieter's connections with the airline, or sitting in coach biting your knees and the person in front of you is resting their head on your lap, eight hours is definitely an eternity. And the only thing marking time are the two tiny arrows mocking their way in little circles on your wrist, enjoying your glance every ten minutes, and laughing inwardly at your predicament.

Until the wheels touch down at your destination. That's when the doors open, the shuffle begins, and the attendants thankfully bid adieu. But the wait at the baggage claim picks up the challenge, leaving your bag as the last one to emerge from the hidden recesses of the terminal until that too is beaten and you head out of the terminal to normality, and life continues.

Natalie and Chris made a quick dash toward the cab stand and waited, again, until it was their turn to seat themselves and announce to the driver their desired final location.

And as they did, the driver nodded in disgust, realizing that his ride only needed to go a few miles rather than into New York or further, and that his renumeration for such a ride was minimal. And with that disgust, he squealed the wheels and sped to the Condor headquarters with the hope of getting back to the terminal to pick up another fare before his time ran out.

Chris and Natalie exited the cab and Chris moved to the driver's window to pay the tab. After a few minutes of discussion, Chris gave the driver a $50 bill and told him to keep the change. The driver acknowledged the generosity, smiled, and drove off. Natalie looked on in shock.

"Why did you give him such a large tip?" she asked.

Chris responded. "You know, he's been waiting for a long time in the line at the terminal for a fare and was hoping that it would be a long one so his time would be well compensated. Well, it wasn't and he was not happy. Now he had to get in the back of the line and wait some more, not making money and using gas. Believe me, he was not a happy camper. So, I gave him a little more than normal to compensate for his loss. He was grateful, and when I told him I worked for the Governor, I may have gotten another vote for my boss. It all comes around."

They stood there, facing each other, both wondering what to do next. Like two teenagers before their first kiss, neither wanted to separate, but both knew they must. So, they waited. And waited. Until Chris muttered the dreaded words. "I have to go." Natalie shook her head in understand.

"You know," she said, "you could stay here with me and drive to the office in the morning," sounding more like a plea than an offer.

Chris understood what she meant, the underlying "Don't go!" of her words. But reality stepped in.

"Thanks for the offer, but I really have to get back to Trenton. I'm sure there is a lot waiting for me, as I am sure there is a lot waiting for you. I need to get an early start, and staying with you would delay that start. So, it is best I get home this evening and get ready for the onslaught. But, believe me when I say that this is not 'good-bye,' this is just a slight pause, a 'see ya later.'" And with that, he bent down and slowly kissed her pouting lips.

She relaxed, knowing he was right, but wishing he wasn't. He slowly walked to his car, got in, and pulled out of the parking. Rolling down his window, he waved as he drove away, blinking his lights like those of a lighthouse gesturing to a safe passage back home.

Natalie quickly drove home and reeled at the stale air that poured out of her apartment as she opened the door. With little hesitation, she opened every window in an attempt to replace the old air with a new, fresh variety, at least as fresh as an apartment next to an airport could be. In a few minutes, order was restored, bags unpacked, mail sorted and a sigh of relief expelled as she realized that she was home. And home is a good place to be.

She picked up the phone and called Margaret, knowing full well she was not at work, but leaving a message to begin her day. "Margaret, just a short call to let you know I am back and will be in the office tomorrow, just not early. Probably around ten or so. Please set up a staff meeting for around one, between one and two, as schedules allow. Also, block off the rest of the day so any issues needing private discussions arising from the staff meeting can be addressed afterwards. Had a good trip, sure you read the papers as to the hostage situation, and the extra week was really something special. I'll fill you in as we have time. Thanks for holding down the fort and I'll see you tomorrow. Have a good night."

All the busy things being taken care of, she sat down for a moment to relax. Just then the phone rang. She picked it up. The voice on the other end said, "Just wanted to let you know that I got home safe and sound. Traffic was a bear, but this bear won to live another day. Are you all settled?"

Natalie smiled. "Yes," she said. "All done and ready to hit the hay, as they say in farmland."

"Me too," replied the voice. "Get a good night's sleep. Oh, and before I forget, thank you for a wonderful week of your time and life and rest assured that I want many more."

Her smile broadened. "Me too," she said, "and thanks for calling. Sleep well, Chris. Till tomorrow."

Her pillow was soft. The sheets were cool. The mattress fit her body. But there was one thing missing.

There was no shoulder to scratch.

Chapter Thirty-Eight

The car pulled into the reserved spot and Natalie got out and walked to the entrance of the Condor building. She entered as the receptionist downstairs rose from her chair behind her desk and said, "Miss Meadows, welcome home. Hope you had a pleasant trip with wonderful memories."

"Thank you," said Natalie. "It is good to be back. Missed this place, but let's see what the day holds for me," as she headed to the stairs leading to the upstairs lobby, anchored by Margaret's desk, and overlooking the airport.

Stairs, she thought. It seems like they add another one each year, just to see how far I can go. Well, here we go.

Stairs. Ever since ancient times stairs have led to the powerful, the strong, the authority, the ruler, the king, or queen, the one who holds the power and demands homage.

Stairs. the path to power, the way to riches, the way to prestige, the way to control over others. A symbol of greatness and a designation, an admission, an acknowledgment, of superiority. We see it all the time, but we don't understand it. But look around and what do you see. Stairs. And more stairs. Stairs leading to the stone sculpture of the Lincoln Memorial. Stairs up monuments and buildings, leading to places of immense value, and power, both to the past and the future.

Natalie thought about that and reflected on her recent visit to Aachen, Germany, once the capital of the Holy Roman Empire and the seat of Charlemagne, the first rule of the Empire.

His throne sits on the second floor of the cathedral. His dignity and power not represented by diamonds, gold, or silver ornaments on his throne. In fact, she remembered it had none of that. In fact, it was ordinary. Nothing special. Four large sheets of iron, two making up the sides of the throne, one upon which he sat, and a fourth making the back of the throne.

She thought one would laugh at it if told it was the throne of the

Holy Roman Empire. Except for one thing. It sat upon a pedestal, a couple of steps above the rest of the chamber, a stark reminder to the others present that here sat the leader of the then-civilized world.

But most important, beneath the simple throne was a passage under the throne through which those lesser kings and rulers of conquered lands were required to crawl through and under, a symbolic gesture of deference to the emperor and an acknowledge of their inferiority to his rule. A simple but eloquent oath of fidelity.

Stairs. The great un-equalizer.

As she reached the stairs, her mind reached back to the first time she ascended. At that time, a young, just graduated college student, she bounded up them like a rabbit, taking two, sometimes three, at a time, and reaching the top with barely the loss of breath. That was a while ago, she thought.

As time went by, the bounding ceased and the dignified, stoic walk up the stairs began. Head high, one step at a time, no need to hold on to the railing, that was for older people, and arriving at the top, a little out of breath, but able to smile and converse without a problem.

And now, the railing that was previously looked at with disdain, has begun to serve its purpose. She walked carefully, watching every step, sliding her hand along the railing to forestall any sideways movement.

It was a nice railing, might as well put it to use, she reasoned, unsure whether to admit she needed it or not. And at the top, with a slight pause to gather her breath, the familiar "Morning, Margaret" greeted the woman seated at the guardian's desk. Margaret immediately rose from her chair, walked over to Natalie, and gave her a big hug.

"Welcome home, Natalie. We missed you, but glad all went well in Germany. The papers covered the story pretty well, we think, but I am sure they, and I, all want to hear what didn't make the pages. But let me show you what I have done to make your day easier." And with that, Margaret began to explain the different piles on her desk, what was immediate, what was not, what was forthcoming, and what could be discarded. Thirty minutes later Natalie was seated at her desk, thumbing through documents Margaret had gathered and assembled. And as usual, time flew with few interruptions.

And after what seemed like thirty minutes, but was over three hours, a slight tap on the door and Margaret said the staff was ready and waiting in the conference room. Natalie stood up from the desk and walked anxiously, wanting to see her friends and fellow workers whom she hadn't seen in what seemed like ages. With a smile on her face and a lilt in her step, she opened the door.

As though on cue, the entire room stood up and what started as a weak background noise grew and grew until the applause drowned out even the planes using the airport. Cheers of "welcome back," "welcome home the hero," and just general approval shouts filled the room. Natalie was a little staggered by the welcome but smiling never the same.

With an exaggerated swagger, she stumbled to her chair and collapsed into its welcoming arms. Looking at her people, she raised her arms, asking for quiet, all the while glowing at the reception. As the noise retreated and the people sat down, a wonderful calm filled the room. If joy could be counted, it would be off the charts.

Natalie looked down both sides of the conference to a sea of smiling faces and wide eyes, waiting to hear more of what went on. But she had other plans, and began to talk.

"You know, or should know, that there were two other Condor employees along with me and both were very helpful in the rescue, one with the planning, and one with the execution. John, from Dick's office was instrumental in the planning of the rescue. His clear, concise, and logical thought process was like a grindstone against which all proposed plans were tested. He obviously was instrumental in choosing the right one. And Stick. You all know Stick, some from long ago, some more recently. But we all know Stick. With his vast knowledge of airplanes, his experience in modifications made to airplanes, and his willingness to join the actual assault on the plane, well, he was Stick. So, I ask that if you see either of them round the area, that you thank them for the effort they put forth on this rescue. For without them, I have serious doubt it would have been successful.

"And I want to add something. I thought about this a long time and had to overcome several obstacles to reach this conclusion, but it is worthy of mention. The Condor team, along with local security officials and German federal law enforcement people, we were all huddled in Dieter's conference room and stymied as to what action we could, or should take. And then a sharp rap came from the door and Dieter, not looking up, said come in. And the answer walked into the room.

"An Army Lieutenant led a group of about six or eight soldiers, both men and women, into the conference room, along with two dogs. The soldiers stayed to the rear of the room while the Lieutenant walked to the front of the room and stopped behind Dieter. He introduced himself, probably not his real name, and said they had been sent over by the US consultant to help where needed and were ready to assist. I won't go into details, would probably get them wrong anyway, but from that moment on a whole new spectrum of ideas began to emerge, with the knowledge that we had the force to implement whatever we decided.

"After the mission was completed, I sat back and remembered, recalled, the actions of this group of soldiers. And from what I have personally seen, I can tell you that we, the United States, has the finest soldiers in the world. They were smart, they were dedicated, they were focused, and they were determined to complete the mission, whatever it took. There were no questions of the Lieutenant, there was no quibbling, there was no arguing among themselves. They each understood what had to be done, their role in it, and they did it. To say the least, I was quite impressed.

"Now I used the Army as an example, because of what I had gone through, but I am sure the same could be said of the Navy, the Air Force, the Marines, the Coast Guard, and even the Border Patrol. So, I ask of you, if you see someone in uniform, go over, thank them for their service and wish them good fortune. And if appropriate, buy them breakfast or lunch, or a beer, but even a sincere Thank You would be appreciated. I know they would like that."

Natalie leaned back in her chair and with a sigh, relaxed. "So, with that being said, the purpose of this gathering is to bring me up to speed with what has been happening in your respective departments. For information that you would rather not share with everyone here, I have set aside the rest of the day for one-on-ones to discuss them. Margaret has filled me in on some of her issues, so we can start with Janet and HR. From there, we will move around the table until all have had a chance to speak. So, Janet, will you please begin."

And the discussions began and the afternoon flew by. When it was over, everyone was a little tired and worn out, but luckily, there were no issues that had to be addressed in private. So, the meeting was adjourned and the shuffle was made to the door. And Natalie went back to her office to finish reading some reports and look at some numbers. A couple of minutes later, Margaret knocked on her door.

"Yes, Margaret?" said Natalie. "What is it?"

Margaret walked over to Natalie's desk holding a business card. "This gentleman has been trying to reach you ever since you left town. Either he or his office has called almost every day to schedule some time with you. I kept putting him off, but apparently the newspapers reported your return, so he has renewed is efforts. Here is his card," she said as she handed it to Natalie.

Natalie looked down at the card which said:

JOHN H. BENOIT
BENOIT-COOK-AND-SANDLER
ATTORNEYS AT LAW
ASSET DISTRIBUTION EXPERTS

Natalie looked at Margaret. "Make an appointment for the day after tomorrow. Tell him I need tomorrow to catch up with things here but the next day, in the afternoon, will work."

Margaret nodded and walked back to her desk to pick up the phone.

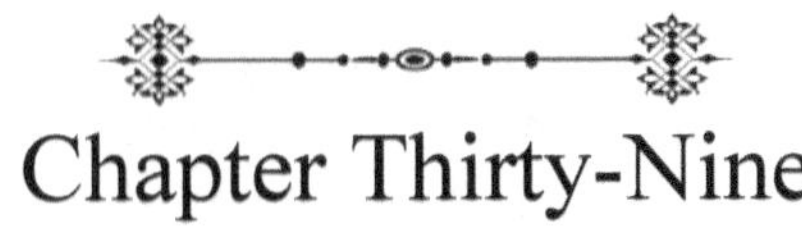

Chapter Thirty-Nine

Margaret tapped slightly on Natalie's door and responded when she waved her in while continuing to delve into some reports in front of her. Upon approaching her desk, Margaret stopped and waited for Natalie to look up.

And when she did, she saw Margaret standing there with a middle-aged gentleman, dressed in a dark blue suit, blending nicely with a lukewarm blue shirt and matching tie. He stood quietly as Margaret introduced him. "Natalie, this is Mr. Benoit, the gentleman who has been looking forward to talking with you."

"Thank you, Margaret," said Natalie and turning to the gentleman, she extended her hand. She continued, "Nice to meet you, Sir. How can I help you today? Oh, please be seated." And with that, they both sat down across from each other.

The gentleman spoke first. "Miss Mathews, it is nice to finally meet you and I appreciate your time. I am here at the request of the former Mrs. Matthews. She has retained my office's services to assist in the transfer of Condor shares in accordance with the agreement made years ago during the court proceedings after your father's death. I trust you remember those proceedings?"

"I do," said Natalie, stiffing slightly at the mention of her father's former wife. "The agreed upon plan was to delay splitting up my father's Condor holdings until such time as his other children reach the age of reason. And the age of reason was, as agreed upon by all the parties, twenty-five years of age. Is that not correct?"

Mr. Benoit nodded in agreement. "That is correct," he affirmed and took some papers out of his briefcase. "I have papers here that my firm has prepared for both parties' signature which reaffirms the agreement and makes way for the transfer to take place. All that is needed is your signature on the two identical documents, one for each child, and I can begin the transfer of the shares from your account to ones established for the children, in accordance with the agreement."

With that, he leaned forward and placed two documents on Natalie's desk and sat back waiting for her signature.

Natalie paused for a moment, looking down at the documents on her desk, refusing to touch them, and hoping they would burst into flames, not because she did not want her siblings to get their fair share of her father's estate, but because she could sense their mother's effort to feather her own nest. With that thought, and a bit of anger, she responded.

"Mr. Benoit, I appreciate the work you have done on behalf of my brother and sister. I will forward these documents to my legal department and have them look at them, along with the proceedings of the court, to ensure they are consistent and fair to all parties. It will probably take a week or so, but they will get back in touch when the review is complete. Again, thank you for your efforts."

"We, eh I had hoped that the documents could be completed today," replied the attorney, "so that the transfer could take place at once. Is a review of the documents by your legal department necessary?"

"Mr. Benoit," replied Natalie. "I have a legal department that has been with me for a long time. Besides providing legal advice, they are friends. If I were to sign these documents without their review it would be a slap in their face, and I would not do that. They will review the documents with me, and we will provide a response as soon as that is done."

The attorney looked fazed, his hope for a quick settlement and signature dashed to the ground. He closed his briefcase, glanced at the documents still lying where he had placed them, and stood up.

"I understand but had hoped for a different response. I will relay your concerns to my client and wait for your review to be completed. Please call me as soon as possible so we can resolve any issues and get this done."

"We will, Mr. Benoit, and again, thank you for your time."

"Margaret, would you please escort Mr. Benoit to the door. Have a good day, Mr. Benoit, and you will be hearing from us."

Margaret and the attorney walked out of the office as Natalie picked up her phone and asked for the legal department.

Chapter Forty

She slid the signed documents across the table to Joan, head of the Condor legal department, and with a weary sigh said, "Glad that is over. How long has this been on the table? Two, maybe three months?"

Joan gathered the papers and slid them into her folder. She crossed her arms and leaned forward onto the table. "Natalie," she said, "it's been a little over six months."

"Whoa, didn't think it would be that difficult."

"Well," said Joan. "The difficult part wasn't the transfer of the Condor stock. The difficult was the reconciliation of the differences in the control of the stock between two hard-headed women. Don't ever do that to me again," she laughed. "I'll retire!"

Natalie chuckled and smiled. "Why? What was the problem? All I wanted was to control the stock to make sure it remained in the family's control. What's so strange about that?"

"Yea," said Joan. "And she wanted control of the stock once the kids got it. And there lies the conflict. But we handled it, not without some compromise, but you got what you wanted, and so did she, both with some compromise. That's how it usually winds up."

"Yea, I agree. Done that in the world of business, but personal issues are a different matter. Seems a little more important and becomes a win/lose situation. But glad it is over, at least for now. I suspect there will be some issues down the road, but we'll handle them one at a time. Anyway, thanks for your help, Joan. I'll put in a good word to your boss. I know her personally."

Joan chuckled getting up from her chair and gathering her things "I appreciate that. Looking forward to bonus time!! So, back to work I go. Let me know if there are any calls from Benoit so I can be in on the discussions. Don't want any misrepresentations on my watch."

She walked to the office door to leave, stopped suddenly and stepped aside as Margaret came into view and said, "You've got visitors."

Margaret stood at the door and watched as Joan left. She turned to Natalie and said, "I found this old guy standing outside and thought you may know him." Stick stuck his head around the corner, smiled, and gingerly entered the office, using his German walking stick not so much as a cane but as a trophy.

Natalie quickly got up from her chair and went over to him, putting her arms around his neck and welcoming him. "Stick, where have you been? I haven't seen you in a couple of weeks, even down the shore. Your table has been empty," she gushed.

Stick smiled and replied, "I have been doing some traveling. Just got back today. Got me a new walking stick," he proclaimed proudly.

Natalie backed off, a little confused. "Where have you been?"

With a single word, the world changed. "Germany."

"What were you doing over there? Is John all right?"

"Better than all right. He and Sophie got married and I was the Best Man. Can you imagine that?"

"What! Nobody told me! How come?"

"It was sudden with little time to plan. He called me and asked me to fly over and be at the wedding. Of course I did, and had no time to tell anyone. but, yes, they are happy about it. Oh, and one other thing."

"Yes?" asked Natalie.

"Sophie is pregnant."

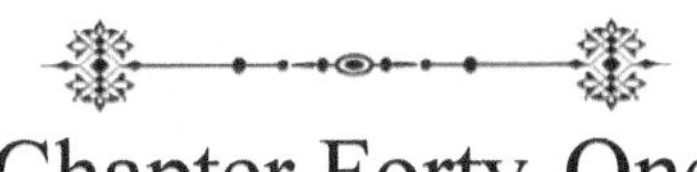

Chapter Forty-One

Time seems to travel in cycles, sometimes slow, sometimes fast, and sometimes it just seems to stop before picking up speed and dashing headlong into the future. And so, it was with Natalie. The pages of the calendar continued to turn and turn, and days went by without even shedding a glimmer of light on the happenings.

"Margaret," called out Natalie. "When you have a chance, we need to talk."

A couple of minutes Margaret stepped into the office and waited.

Natalie started to speak. "You know, it's about time that we had another—"

"No," said Margaret.

Natalie looked surprised. "No?" she questioned. "No what?"

"No. Just no," replied Margaret.

"You don't even know what I was going to say."

"Oh yes, I do. I look at the calendar every day, just as you do."

"And you know what I was going to say?"

"Yes. And no."

"OK, so what was I going to say?"

Margaret, looking smug, replied, "You were going to say that it is about time we had another company-wide celebration, like the one twenty-five years ago, and you wanted me to organize it like I did the last time."

"No."

"Margaret," said Natalie with a sigh, "how long have you worked here?"

"Longer than you, my dear. Remember, I was your father's secretary and actually hired you to work for me. My, how things have changed," she whispered with a smile.

Natalie leaned back in her chair, clasped her fingers and raised her hands above her head. "Margaret," she said. "You have a natural smartness, a natural feeling for what is right and wrong. Why haven't you used that, gotten ahead in business, gone to college and—"

"Oh, I went to college," she paused, "at least for one day," said the secretary. "Learned a lot."

Natalie leaned forward. "How can you learn a lot in one day? College usually takes years, usually four years. What can you learn in one day?"

Margaret moved slowly toward Natalie's desk, pulled out a chair from the table alongside and sat down.

"You know, I thought the same thing when I was your age. I figured it was going to be a long four years and had girded myself for the long haul. Not happy about it, but willing to take the plunge. And then I went to my first class. It was Psychology or Business Psychology, or something like that, don't remember the exact name, but it was kind of like an entry-level class for business. All of us new students were seated and waiting for the professor to show up, and eventually he did. We waited with bated breath to expand our minds and learn, learn anything, just learn.

"The professor put his briefcase on the table in the front of the room, took out a book and placed it on the podium where he stood. 'Students,' he said, 'Please turn to page 254 in your text.'

"We all did as he asked, wondering why he started on page 254 and not at the beginning of the book. Well, we were all surprised when page 254 turned out to be blank. There was not a word or note or anything on the page. Absolutely nothing. Needless to say, there was quite a murmur going around until one student asked why we should be looking at a blank page.

"And here, Natalie, was the essence of college education.

"The professor looked around at the students, looked down at page 254, and looked back up again. With words that shook the class, he carefully spoke. 'You see, page 254 is blank. Nothing there. And that is because all you need to know, all you need to succeed in life, all you need to be happy in life, all of that, is already inside you. It is not on this page, nor any other pages you may read. You already have it. All you must do is be willing to seek it, to look for it within yourself, and when, and if you find it, you will have all the knowledge, skill, and happiness you want and need. Just remember, page 254 is your guide.'

"With that, I packed up my things and walked to the back of the room and started to leave. The professor asked me why I was leaving, and I said that I had learned all I needed to know. He just nodded.

"As I was leaving, I turned back to the professor and said, 'And I expect to get an 'A' for this class.'

The professor said, 'Who are you, I don't even know your name.'

I laughed a little and said, "That's your assignment for the rest of the semester. Good luck,' and walked out and never looked back."

"Well," asked Natalie smiling, "did you get an 'A' for the class?"

"A+," said Margaret. "Best lesson I ever learned."

"Oh, and speaking of lessons, there is one waiting outside to see you. Benoit. John Benoit."

"Ah," said Natalie, "the attorney. Show him in, oh, and call—"

"I already did. Joan will be here shortly."

Natalie just shook her head in awe.

Chapter Forty-Two

John Benoit walked into the office followed almost immediately by a gasping Joan struggling to get there before the meeting began. "Mr. Benoit, nice to see you again. A surprise. I hope this is a more pleasant meeting than the previous one which took up almost six months of my legal staff's time."

The attorney smiled and extended his hand. "Good to see you Natalie, and you also Joan. Hope things are going well with both of you,"

"Please sit down," said Natalie as she moved to the small conference table in her office. Joan moved to sit next to Natalie and opened a pad to take notes as Benoit sat down.

"Well," he said. "This is partially business and partially personal, but all professional. I want you to know that I have been retained by the formal Mrs. Matthews to represent her two children in filing a Board of Directors meeting request for Condor Airlines, to be held as soon as possible. As you know, any Board member can file such a request and after this meeting I will be going over to the Bank to submit such a request to Sharon, the official of the bank, who acts as your non-voting Secretary of the Board for Condor. In turn, she will be sending out official notices of the requested meeting and coordinating the date. However, I wanted you to know this before-hand so the notice would not be a surprise."

"John," said Joan. "As I am sure you are aware, such a request outside of the normal Board meetings requires a proposed agenda to give Board members a heads-up as to what is to be discussed. Will you be giving that to Sharon along with the meeting request?"

"Yes, I will," said the attorney, "and that is why I came over here before going to the bank."

The attorney hesitated.

"The agenda item to be submitted calls for a vote on replacing you, Natalie, as the Chairperson of the Board and the appointment of a new President of Condor. That is the only item on the agenda."

A quiet still engulfed the room as if a vacuum had sucked all the air out, leaving only a void of questions and confusions surrounding the two women. Natalie stood slowly, extended her hand to the attorney, and quietly said, "Thank you, Mr. Benoit, for your coming over today. I appreciate it."

The attorney shook Natalie's hand and stonily walked to the door. "Ladies," he said, "have a good day."

Natalie looked down at Joan who was slowly shaking her head side to side. "Looks like we have some work to do, Joan. Let's think about this for a while and get together later today to formulate some type of plan."

Joan nodded in agreement, gathered her belongings, and headed for the door. "Never a dull moment," she said as she disappeared around the corner.

Chapter Forty-Three

The gavel tapped gently on the conference table as Sharon, the non-voting Secretary of the Board of Directors as appointed by Condor's partner bank, tried to bring the meeting to order. In response, the attendees muted their voices and turned their attention to the Secretary.

"This meeting of the Condor Airlines Board of Directors shall come to order. This meeting was requested by Members of the Board to bring the following agenda item to vote:

"Be it resolved that the present Chairperson of the Condor Airlines Board of Directors, Ms. Natalie Matthews, having lost the confidence of the Board, shall be removed from such position and be replaced by another, who shall be elected by the Board by a clear majority of those voting in accordance with the by-laws of the Board.

"This request for the Board meeting and the proposed agenda item is both in accordance with the Board's by-laws. Notification, as required, was sent to the addresses on record of the Board members in the required time period to allow for attendance. I shall now pass around an attendance verification sheet for placement in the official minutes of this meeting. Please sign next to your name or company's name and address and pass around. After verification, we shall begin with voting on the agenda."

The attendance record began its journey around the table. Natalie was the first to sign. Seated behind her was Joan, head of legal overseeing the meeting on behalf of Natalie. Next sat Dick Russell, head of operations and next to him was Bill Snyder, Director of Maintenance, both of Condor.

Around the corner of the table sat Ron's two other children, Ronald Jr., and Elizabeth, now both holders of Condor stock. The children's mother sat behind them. Next to them sat John Benoit, their attorney. Three other chairs sat empty as the sign-in sheet passed them by and returned to Sharon.

"OK," said Sharon. "It appears we are ready to vote. Just a reminder that an 'Aye' vote agrees with the proposal that Natalie Matthews be removed from her position as Chairperson of the Board, and a 'Nay' vote agrees with Natalie Matthews continuing as Chairperson of the Board. The quantity of your votes will be equivalent to the percentage of company shares that you own., thus a Board member owning five percent of the company stock will get five votes. I will keep a running count of the votes and announce the status after each party votes. Natalie, with eighteen votes, you are first to register your vote."

Natalie sat straight up in her chair and with a clear voice voted "Nay."

Sharon stated, "Nays are 18, Ayes are 0."

Dick Russell, Director of Operations of Condor, with ten votes, was the next one to vote and he also voted "Nay."

Sharon stated, "Nays are 28. Ayes are 0."

Bill Snyder, Director of Maintenance of Condor, also with ten votes, voted "Nay."

Sharon stated, "Nays are 38. Ayes are 0."

Looking at Ronald Jr., Sharon waited for his seventeen votes. With a sideways look to his mother, he responded with "Aye."

Sharon paused, then stated, "Nays are 38, Ayes are 17.

A stir made its way around the table as eyes turned to Elizabeth, also with seventeen votes. After moment of hesitation, she voted "Aye."

Sharon softly stated, "Nays are 38, Ayes are 34."

Sharon spoke, "Let me explain something before we go on. The total votes so far, eighteen, seventeen, and seventeen is equal to the fifty-two percentage of common stock owned by Mr. Ron Matthews before his demise and reflects the division of such stock by the courts during the probate hearing. The one additional percentage given to Natalie Williams is in recognition of her accomplishments as President of Condor Airlines during the period between Mr. Matthews' death and the coming of age of his younger children, Ron Jr. and Elizabeth. Unless there are questions, we shall resume the voting." Seeing none, she proceeded.

Sharon looked at the first empty chair. Seeing no one seated she asked if there was anyone in the room representing JHB Inc., the registered shareholder and member of the Board. All was quiet for a moment, until a hand was raised.

Sharon looked surprised, as did Natalie and Joan. "Yes sir, what is it?" asked Sharon.

"I am the representative of JHB Inc.," said the attorney, John Benoit.

"I thought you were here representing Ron and Elizabeth Matthews? I don't understand."

"I am," responded Benoit. "However, I am also the owner and principal stockholder of JHB Inc. As such, I have the voting rights of the company. Here are my credentials to prove my standing," he said handing over confirming documents.

Sharon looked at the documents, one by one, and placed them in the middle of the table. "It appears they are legitimate. They are even confirmed by officials of my own bank. However, should anyone care to review them, please do."

Joan stood and looked at the documents. After a minute, she looked at Natalie and nodded in the affirmative. No one else moved.

"Mr. Benoit, it appears your status with JHB Inc. is verified and thus your membership on this Board is confirmed. Please vote your fourteen votes."

The attorney starred, first at Natalie, then at Joan. With a clear voice he voted "Aye."

Sharon hesitated, and with a note of sorrow in her voice, announced, "Nays are 38, Ayes are 48."

It was as though the room was divided into two separate compartments, one full of smiles and cheerful exchanges, the other slowly sinking into the abyss of despair. It was not a pretty sight.

Bang! went the door of the conference room, as voices could be heard on the other side. Bank! It went again. "Someone open the damn door!" said a stern male voice yelling, wanting to get in.

"I told you we should have taken the elevator, but no, you had to walk," decried a female voice outside.

Unsure of what he would find on the other side, Mr. Benoit opened the door and immediately stepped aside. Coming into the room was a wheelchair occupied by Stick and reluctantly pushed by Margaret. She looked around the room and its occupants, now confused by their attendance, and lightly smacked Stick on the back of his head. "I told you we were going to be late," she said sternly. She looked at Sharon, whom she knew from previous meetings and apologized for being late.

"We would have been on time had this old coot not demanded to walk up the stairs with his damn walking stick instead of taking the elevator," she snorted.

"Well," retorted Stick, "I made it, didn't I!"

"Yea, and I had to ask a young gentleman to help me get the wheelchair into the elevator. Thank goodness he was walking past."

"You know, you old man, if you were my husband, I would give you poison!"

Stick turned and looked at her and with feigned distain, and replied, "And to quote a distinguished Prime Minister, if I was your husband, Madam, I would gladly take it."

The tension in the room snapped like an over-stretched rubber band.

The gavel fell to the floor, laughter filled the room, and Sharon buried her head in the palms of her hands, banging them on the conference table, wondering when and how she had lost control of the meeting.

Stick turned to Margaret. "Push me over there where the two chairs are. You can sit in one alongside of me."

Sharon tried to regain composure. "Those are for voting members of the Board of Directors only, not for you or Margaret. There are chairs along the wall if you want to watch, assuming none of the Board members has any objection."

Stick seemed amused. "What names are on those chairs?"

Sharon looked a little perturbed. "I don't have the exact names, but the attendance list identified them as Anonymous 1 and Anonymous 2. That's all I have. They have not yet shown up, in fact my attendance records from the past several meetings, going back over the years, have not indicated them showing up for any of the meetings. However, we must plan in case they appear. So, please take any of the seats along the wall so we can get on with the voting."

"Good," said Stick. "I'll stay in this wheel thing so you can remove one of the chairs." And handing over a folder of documents, he continued, "These are the documents signed by your own George Franklin, who was President of your bank when Condor first started. I didn't want to be identified with the airline, for reasons I can't remember, so I asked to be identified as Anonymous 1. And Ron

Matthews gave me several shares of stock as a thank you for helping him get started and sticking with him when things were tough. And believe me, there were times like that. My stock position has grown, as with splits and stuff I don't understand, so I believe I belong here."

With a pause, he ended, "I'll take my place at the table now."

Margaret pushed Stick to the conference table, removing the empty chair so he could take its place. She then sat down next to him in the other chair.

"Margaret," said Sharon, "is your story pretty much the same?"

"Oh, I'm sorry, here are my similar documents as Stick's except I chose the name Anonymous 2 because Mister Big Shot over here had to be number one. He and I have held these shares for many, many years, getting a check every now and then, but having no use for them until now. I too would like to take my place at the table and vote."

Sharon checked the documents, and as before, offered them to the attendees for their review. Mr. Benoit scanned over them and accepted them with the caveat that further investigation may prove them invalid and thus render the vote invalid, causing a second vote. With that noted, Sharon explained the voting procedures to the new members and resumed the count.

"Anonymous 1, with ten votes, how do you vote?"

Stick quickly replied, "I vote Nay."

Sharon announced, "The Nays have 46, the Ayes have 48."

"Margaret, it is your turn as Anonymous 2 to cast your five votes. Please do so."

Margaret looked Natalie straight in the eyes, smiled, and said, "I vote Nay."

Sharon announced, with a sign of relief, "The Nays have 51. The Ayes have 48. In accordance with the by-laws of this Board, the proposal is defeated and there will be no change in the position of Chairperson of the Board."

"Wait, wait," yelled Mr. Benoit. "That only adds up to 99 Percent. Where are the remaining shares?"

Sharon held up a sealed envelope. "The remaining shares are the property of the Bank, as payment for services, such as my being here, given to the Bank by Ron Williams upon the issuance of public stock. It was to be used in case of a tie in voting. That is not the case, so it will remain sealed and returned to the Bank for future use.”

“There being no further business, this meeting is adjourned. Thank you all for your attendance and good wishes for the future.”

The gavel banged once on the table.

Natalie and Joan quickly walked to Natalie’s office. “Please shut the door, Joan. I want to tell you something.”

Joan did as asked and turned to Natalie.

“Joan, I want you to get hold of my broker with instructions to buy all Condor stock available and to do so for the next year unless sooner instructed otherwise.” With a pause, she continued, “This is something I never want to go through again.”

Joan turned and left. Natalie looked around at her life contained within the four walls of her office, reflecting on each object as a symbol of the happiness it brought her. But one thing was missing.

She picked up the phone and frowned when the answering machine responded. With a single touch, she forwarded past the message and left one of her own.

“Chris, we won. I miss you.”

Chapter Forty-Four

All was quiet on this Saturday evening as Natalie entered from Beach Bum's open patio and headed to the familiar table in the corner. A few people were sitting at the bar, and fewer yet were at the tables outside.

Summer was over and the locals had reclaimed their spots as the tourists moved away regaling themselves as to the splendid summer they had had at the shore.

The bartender waved, recognizing her as a regular, and prepared a diet Coke with a lemon. He motioned for one of the servers to take it over to the Stammtisch table, getting it there as Natalie sat down and starred across the wooden divide at Stick, who leaned back on his chair and smiled that crooked little smile he did when he wanted to say "I told you," She raised the Coke in a salute, took a sip, and said, "Nice to see you again."

"Stick," she said. "I'm getting too old for this stuff. It was not fun this morning. I was close to losing the dearest thing to my heart and if it weren't for friends like you and Margaret, it would be gone. Forever. It was not fun."

Stick looked at her fondly and spoke softly. "You know, Natalie, I have been with this airline since its inception. I worked with your dad, helped him through some tough spots both in the business world and in personal life. He and I, and a few others who you know, realized a dream, a dream that I really didn't even know existed till he found me one day. A dream I could not really appreciate because of his early departure from this life. And I owed my own life to him because of his faith in me. And when he left, I thought the dream was going to end. But then you, you came along. this beautiful young woman, freshly out of college, with little or no knowledge of any business, let alone the airline business, and strapped the harness to your tiny shoulders and pulled us out of the doldrums of despair and into realm of not only sanity, but success. And we all jumped onto the cart and enjoyed what you gave us. Both then, and now, as we spend our leisure years. Perhaps, my dear, it is time for you to sit back and enjoy your success and look forward to the next chapter in your life.”

Natalie sat back and reflected on what Stick had just said. It had been a long day, and many long years, and perhaps he was right in his suggestion. Something to mull over.

“You know, Stick, you may have something there. But I have a slight problem. I don’t know anyone who could take the reins and do the job. My father and I, along with you and the other members of the old team, have invested too much in Condor to let it go downhill. Just not going to let it happen. So, I haven’t even looked, though I just don’t know anyone who could, or would, do the job. I think I may just be stuck with it.”

“Yes, you do,” said Stick. “You just haven’t looked hard enough.”

Natalie sat there wondering what Stick meant when a hard hand laid itself on her shoulder. Startled, she turned around and gasped. “Chris, what are you doing here?” she asked with her concern molting into pleasure.

“Well, got a message about something being missed so figured I would check up on it. This odd feeling led me down here and when I saw your car parked outside the bungalow and no one answered the door, I figured you were here at your office annex. And, lo and behold, lookie what I found.”

Natalie placed her hand on Chris’ and smiled. “Thanks for realizing my need. Please, sit, join Stick and me. We were just solving the world’s problems. And failing miserably I might add.”

Chris sat and the three of them, interrupted only by additional coke and beer, laughed, and joked their way through the next hour or so. The relief valve had been opened.

“Well,” said Stick, rising from his chair. “Got an early day tomorrow, need to get some shut eye.”

Natalie looked wondered. What did this retired old man have going on that he needed to worry about sleep? “What’s going on?” she asked with a questioning look.

“Got a flight to catch in the morning. Going to Germany.”

“Whoa, what?” said Chris. “What’s that about?” echoing Natalie’s thoughts. “How come?”

Stick looked at them both. “You know Sophie is pregnant, right? Well, she is getting close, and I want to be there with John when she gives birth. The child, after all, is my first grandchild and I want to be there. Nothing strange about that, is there?"

Both Natalie and Chris nodded in agreement. They too stood up, wished Stick a good flight and offered to do whatever they could while he was away.

"Does Margaret know where you're going?" asked Natalie.

"Yep," replied Stick. "She's going too. Somebody has got to take care of this old coot. Can't do it by myself," he laughed.

Natalie and Chris looked at each other in a wondering fashion. "Well," said Natalie, "have a good trip, stay safe, give our best to John and Sophie and the grandchild, oh, do you know if it is boy or girl?"

"Don't know, and, neither do they as they want it to be a surprise. Like all parents, all they want is a healthy baby."

"Understand. Well, again, have a good trip. Let us know if we can do anything and looking forward to pictures."

They shared hugs and went their own way.

SIX MONTHS PASSES

"Look," said Stick beaming, as he sat down at the table. "I got some pictures from John and Sophie." Beaming, he extended the photos across the wooden divide, separating them out so they could all be seen at the same time. A tiny little face, eyes barely opened, looked up at the wonderous world coming into focus, not knowing what ever to expect, nor evening thinking of what lies ahead.

Stick pointed to the little fingers, squeezing together as though trying to grasp something, perhaps the entire world, or at least what she knew of the world. Little did she know.

"How they doing?" asked Natalie. "Everything going all right?"

"Yea," Stick replied, "a little hectic now with the little one and accommodations are tight, but overall, John says they are doing fine. He did sound a little tired, probably because of Shatzie, but work seems to be less interesting. Don't know, the novelty of working overseas has worn off. Time will tell."

Natalie frowned, as if questioning herself. "Shatzie? What, or who, is Shatzie?" she asked.

Stick laughed. "That's the nickname they gave the baby. It stands for 'treasure' or 'darling.' It's a form of endearment and has kind of become her nickname. It's funny, they told me her real name and I can't remember it. Everyone calls her Shatzie, even the neighbors. Kind of cute."

"When are they coming back to the States?" asked Chris.

"Don't know for sure. They have talked about it, but Sophie's Mom is getting along in age and so they want to stay around for a while. But John misses being here, with his old crew and haunts. Kind of a toss-up."

ONE YEAR PASSES

Natalie and Chris sat on the worn porch of the bungalow, a small metal portable fire-pit sending waves of warm air in their direction while warding off the cool ocean breeze.

"Chris, have you ever thought of marriage?"

"Yes," laughed Chris, "but not much."

"No," said Natalie leaning forward. "I mean about us, you know, getting married?"

Chris looked Natalie straight in her eyes. "Now, why would we want to do that?"

"Just seems like the thing to do, after all this time. Why not?"

Chris took his time to answer. He obviously had given the question some thought. With the sigh of a convicted killer going to his execution, he responded.

"Natalie, I remember the first time I saw you. That was at the convention center where we met to discuss your buying my mom's house when she moved on. And I remember John Nash saying as he was ushered out the door, 'Don't let this one get away!!'"

And for years I have done my damndest to follow his advice. And in doing so, I have enjoyed the most wonderful years of my life. Just you and me. And the world we live in, with all its pleasures, rewards, and yes, sorrows and tears. But through it all, we, you and I, have managed to hang on and keep moving forward. And we have done so without a piece of paper. It has all been based on mutual trust, mutual admiration of the accomplishments of the other, mutual understanding of the wants and desires of the other, and, perhaps above all, friendship, for without that there is nothing. And a piece of paper is not going to add to that. I feel strongly about that. But I am not going to let 'this one get away' so if that is your desire, I am in."

Natalie gazed at Chris, sipped a bit of wine, reached over and stroked his cheek with her soft hand and said, "I love you."

Chapter Forty-Five

Time. That mythical being that seems to surround us all, yet remains elusive in touch, in feel, in all we do. It affects all it comes in contact with and yet we don't know how to control it. In fact, it controls us, causes us to do certain things, punishes us when we fail to do others, but seldom rewards us for doing things which contribute to the good of all concerned. It hangs over our heads like a scimitar waiting to fall and end it all.

Time. We adore it to such an extent that it has become a lexicon with our own language. Phrases such as "I need time" or "Alone time" or "Time will tell" permeate our conversations to such as extent we don't even know they are used. And yet the concept of time has been around forever, only to have been identified by different situations or occurrences.

Ancient civilizations used the position of the stars and the location of the moon to identify when to plant crops. The flooding of the Nile reminded the Egyptians of the need to pray and thank the gods for their blessings. In fact, it was Sosigenes, the court astronomer during the reign of Cleopatra, who replaced the lunar calendar with one based on the sun, giving us twelve months for each year.

But each year was different, requiring Pope Gregory XIII, in 1582, to adjust the calendar to include the leap year and bring things in line with the sun. And we still use the Gregorian calendar today to guide our days and activities and remind us of the past. Scientific advancements in astrology and electronics took that day and divided it into hours, then minutes, and finally seconds. So, time becomes the duration between Event A and Event B and recognized by all as such.

Except some.

Stick slowly walked through the door of Natalie's office and quietly moved toward the desk. Natalie glanced up from the pile of papers scattered before her and raised a finger, asking for a minute to finish what she was doing. Stick sat down in front of the desk.

A minute later Natalie looked up from the pile of papers, now pushed aside for later review, and looked at Stick like, "OK, what are you doing here?"

Stick leaned forward and looked Natalie straight in her eyes. "John is coming home this month."

An eerie silence blanketed the room, now void of all sound and instead filled with questions.

"What?" said Natalie.

"John is coming home this month."

"Why? How come? How long is he staying?" Natalie asked in frustration. "Why didn't I know about this?"

"He just told me this morning. He called to let me know and I figured you would want to know."

Natalie hesitated. "How long is he staying?" she asked.

"He's not going back. He, Sophie and Shatzie are leaving Germany and moving back here for good. He said it was time."

"Wait. He's only been there for, what, a year, perhaps a little over a year? Why so soon?"

"Natalie," reminded Stick, "it's been over three years since the hostage situation, and he's been in Germany since that time. Things have changed over in Condor. Dieter is retiring and he thought it was time to move on. Anyway, no firm date yet as he needs to wrap things up. But I'll let you know."

"I know Dieter is retiring. I offered the position to John, but he turned it down. Not sure why."

"He turned it down because it would have been a permanent job, and he wasn't sure he wanted that. Even then he was thinking about returning. Then when Jacob got the job, he was sure he wanted to move. He and Jacob do not get along and he couldn't work for him. Just strengthened his resolve to move. He wanted to bring Sophie, and especially Shatzie, to the States and have them settle here. He thought it would be better for them."

"What do you think, Stick? Is it better?"

"I don't know. Everybody must move on at some point in their life. but each must make their own choice. So, for him, I don't know. I knew when it was time for me, and you, even you, will face that point in your life. We each are different, with different views, different goals, and different choices. To each their own."

Stick got up and turned to leave. ""I'll let you know when I hear something," he said as he waved goodbye.

Natalie sat there for a moment, stunned by what she had just learned and even more so by Stick's comments about moving on. A couple of minutes went by, and she called out to Margaret, "Get hold of HR, Janet, and ask her to come up for a minute. Want to discuss something with her."

Chapter Forty-Six

"Yo boss, waz up," mimicked Janet learning on the door jamb, a pen extending between her fingers like a long cigarette holder. "Wats U got?"

Natalie looked up and laughed. "What are you doing?" she asked, her fingers intwined around the back of her head.

"Jus tryinn to blend in wit da Jersey crowd. Ya know wat I meen?"

"OK, well blend in elsewhere, we have some talking to do," said Natalie as she smiled and moved to the table.

Janet recognized this as something important. Common items, business items, were normally discussed across Natalie's desk. Sitting at the table meant a discussion of equals, a topic for and requesting individual input before arriving at a decision.

It was a time for reflection, interaction, back and forth parrying, and freedom to express one's thoughts, opinions, and ideas. It was time to stop playing and start working.

The two women sat across from each other, Janet waiting for Natalie to start the discussion, not even knowing the topic. With a sign, Natalie leaned back, her eyes kind of staring at the office ceiling before descending on Janet.

"Janet," said Natalie, "The time has come. I need your help. I need you to draft a job description for the position of Vice President of Condor Airlines."

Janet looked directly across the table at the woman who had led the company for many wonderful and successful years. "Are you serious? Do you really mean that?" With a sense of anxiety, she waited.

"Yes," said Natalie softly. "I do."

As if a huge firecracker had exploded under Janet's chair, she jumped up, slammed her open hand on the table and with the exuberance of a young child at Christmas, yelled "Yes! Yes! Yes!" as she swirled around like a ballerina.

Natalie was stunned. She didn't know what to make of the sudden outburst. She stared at Janet as it she had just met her, just been introduced. This was somebody she had not seen before, even after a few beers. To say it was a surprise would be a complete understatement.

Janet saw Natalie's confusion, her lack of understanding of what had just happened. She sat down slowly and quietly. "Sorry," she said, returning to her normal stoic self. "Didn't mean to react that way."

"Well, apparently you approve of the action. Do you care of explain why?"

Janet hesitated a short while and then called for Margaret to join them. Margaret, who had been listening at her desk, quickly entered the office and sat down at the table. Janet and Margaret looked at each other as though revealing the ere-to-for secret of the universe.

Janet began. "You remember that years ago when you first took over the company after the death of your father, one of the first things you did was to institute an intern program, the purpose of which was to select and train individuals who were felt to have the potential to take over key positions within the company. The thought being let's get somebody new whom we could train in the way we do things, who could be indoctrinated into the Condor culture, who could develop relationships with other interns, all with the intent of ensuring the continuation of the Condor brand and the Condor way of doing things."

"I remember," said Natalie. "It was not received very well."

"No," said Janet. "It was not received well at all. Sitting senior executives saw the program as a way to remove them from their positions and replace them with a younger crop of managers. They saw all their hard work and livelihood being stripped away. No, it was not welcomed at all."

"But that has changed," she continued. "The executives began to realize that one of their responsibilities was to train, to groom, to get ready, someone to take their place, being through the normal process of retirement or some unfortunate circumstance. The need was present, and it was part of their job to fill that need. And so, they took to the task and today we have one of the most successful intern programs in the industry and it stands as the model for other airlines to follow. All because of your realization that we are not going to be around forever.

"I'm sure you know, I have a monthly meeting with all the department heads and senior manager just for the sake of hearing thoughts, complaints, ideas, etc. that have come up through the ranks to them and they feel should be shared and discussed with HR. It works well and we all kind of look forward to the meetings.

"Several months ago, almost a year, one of the discussions turned to the intern program and some of the tweaks we could implement to make it better. One of the Directors, forget who, bought up the subject that all the departments had an intern program, yet there was one department, one individual, who had not followed her own advice. One lone wolf who still insisted that she was going to be here forever. One holdout."

Natalie listened carefully, and realizing where the conversation was headed, leaned back with a sign of resignation, and said, "That be me."

"Yes," said Janet. "That be you."

"So, when you asked me to draft a job description for a Vice President, I realized that you had finally decided, for whatever reason, that your successor needed to be selected, groomed, and readied to take over Condor. The need for this was never more evident than when you were in Germany and decisions had to be made on some subjects. Your professional department heads met several times to develop a course of action, consistent with what you would have chosen, but that is not the way it is supposed to operate. Someone must be in charge and your absence showed even more the need for that person."

Natalie now understood the demonstrative show of excitement Janet had displayed. "How long before you can have a draft job description?" asked Natalie.

"Well, today is Wednesday, maybe by Friday, but Monday for sure."

"So soon?" questioned the CEO of Condor.

"Yes," said Janet. "Since that monthly meeting I have been working on such a description, coordinating it with some department heads to get their opinions in anticipation of this moment. It's not done, but close. As I said, I can have a draft, a rather good draft, for you on Monday at the latest."

Natalie rose from the table, suggesting the meeting was done.

"Let's do it."

Janet and Margaret made their way out of the office, high fiving excitedly at the results. Janet turned to Natalie just before exiting, "Ya dun good, boss," and sashayed out the door.

Chapter Forty-Seven

The day and week were about to end, and Margaret was clearing her desk getting ready to head out for the weekend. She grabbed her purse and started for the door to Natalie's office when she heard a noise coming from the opening elevator door.

She turned and looked, hesitated a bit and then with a big smile, knocked on Natalie's door and announced, "I think you have some people who want to see you."

Natalie looked up frowning wondering who it could be this late on a Friday afternoon. "OK," she said, "show them in."

With a silly grin on their faces, John and Sophie walked through the door. "Oh, my word!" screamed Natalie as she jumped out from behind her desk, ran over and hugged them both. "What are you doing here? Stick said you were coming back but I had no word it would be this soon. How are you?" said asked anxiously.

"Doing fine," said John. "Things just kind of fell into place so we left early. It was a long trip but we made it."

"Yea, you folks look a little bit tired. Can I get you anything?"

"No thanks," said Sophie. "We just got off the plane and wanted to say hello before heading down to Stick's. We're staying at his house for a while till we find our own place. It should be just fine."

"Yea, will be a little tight with Stick and the three of you with only two bedrooms," Natalie said looking around. "Wait, where is the little one?" looking around, suddenly realizing their daughter was not with them.

Sophie and John both laughed. "Dad, it's time," they spoke to the office door.

It was as if a little bit of sunshine had just arrived. The clouds had disappeared, the wind escaped, and this smiling little angel walked through the door, glancing up to Mommy and Daddy and floated to Natalie. She stopped, glanced again at Mommy and Daddy, turned and looked at Natalie and with a gracious, but somewhat unsteady curtsy she said, "Hello Miss Natalie. It's nice to see you."

The whole north Atlantic icecap melted. Tears of joy formed in her eyes as Natalie reached out to touch the little angel, first touching her hand, then, with an I-don't-care attitude, grasped her in a lovingly hug. "Oh, it's so good to see you also, ah, ah—" as she turned to John looking, questioning, for a name.

"Shatzie," said John.

"Shatzie, wow what a beautiful name," Natalie said to the little girl.

"It means treasure when you talk German. Mommy and Daddy say it's my nickname," said the angel.

"Can I call you Shatzie?" asked Natalie.

The little girl looked at her parents who both nodded in the affirmative. "Yes, my parents said you can."

"Great," replied Natalie. "I like that. That is a great nickname. Do you have a different name, a real name?"

"Yes, I have a real name. Mommy and Daddy named me Ingrid."

The flood gates of yesteryear crashed open at the sound of her mother's name and Natalie dropped to the floor with crossed legs, arms reaching out for history.

Her mind raced back to little tricycles squealing around the neighborhood, the mothers watching, the quiet walks to the neighborhood store with their little baskets piled high with vegetables picked out under the watchful eye of the mothers, the closing of the school bus doors as years slipped, the only constant being the mothers waving and the whispered, "I love you," through the bus window.

And even the final, "I'll be right back," as she went to the hospital restroom before her mother entered Ron's room and changed the way the world was going.

With a sign and a tortured smile Natalie quietly responded, "I like that name too. That's one of my favorites."

Time stood still, until reality burst upon the scene.

"Well," said John, "we best be going, right Dad?"

"Yep," said Stick. "Traffic is going to be a little rough this time of the day." He reached down to help Natalie to her feet as Ingrid grabbed her other hand to also help. It was a touch Natalie thought she would never, ever forget.

Margaret, who had been standing there the whole time, walked over to the little girl and with a smile, said, "Come with me. I want to show you a secret with the elevator," and led little Ingrid out of the office.

The adults, what was left of them, said their goodbyes, and made plans for the weekend as Natalie was heading to the shore also.

"Natalie," said a little voice from just outside the office. "Please come see us. I like you."

Chapter Forty-Eight

Ring!! Ring!!

Her arm snaked out from under the covers, searching for the cause of the disturbance while knocking the deliberately-turned-off alarm clock to the floor. "Hello," said the mumbled voice.

"Well, don't you sound charming this morning."

"Chris!! Good morning, where are you?"

"Just leaving now, should be there in about an hour. Keep the coffee hot for me. Till later."

"OK, see you when you get here," said Natalie, as she bent to pick up the undamaged alarm clock and place it back on the table. With a small stretch, she crawled out of bed and went to wash her face and wake up before starting the coffee.

An hour later, Chris pulled up. They sat on the porch sipping the hot liquid and chatted about almost anything. "Where were you last night, thought maybe you would join me down here."

"Was planning on it, but then got an unexpected invitation by the Governor to attend a dinner at the mansion hosting some of the less supportive legislators. The dinner was nice, but not as opulent as Beach Bum's, which I would have much preferred attending, but we all have our burdens to bare."

"Yea, life is tough, believe me. But relax, we are meeting Stick, John, Sophie, and Shatzie there for lunch this afternoon so you can enjoy what you missed last night."

"Shatzie?"

"Yep, Shatzie. That's the little one's nickname. Means treasure and, believe me, is quite appropriate. But you will see."

A few more sips and it was time to clean up and get ready for lunch. They went inside, did what needed to be done and walked down to Beach Bum's.

Stick was already there, sitting at his usual table and waved as they walked in. Tiny saw them also, and waved as he carried dishes back to the kitchen. They sat, got comfortable, and chatted a bit waiting for the others before ordering.

A couple of minutes later John, Sophie, and Shatzie walked in, looked around the restaurant and spotted Stick and Natalie and Chris seated at the corner table. Chris stood to welcome the newly-arrived trio and gazed as the little girl pulled her father's hand, in a hurry to get there.

"Hi, Natalie," said the little voice, ignoring the others seated at the table. "How are you?"

"I'm doing well," said Natalie smiling. "Did you get a good night's sleep?"

"I did, but the water made a lot of noise that kept me awake for a while. But it was good."

"Shatzie, this is Chris. He is a, ah, ah, a friend of mine," said Natalie motioning to the man sitting next to her.

Chris smiled and Stick laughed aloud.

"What are you laughing at, Grandpa?" asked Shatzie.

"Nothing," said Stick. "Just coughing."

At that moment, Tiny walked over to the table to take their order. "Morning all, hope the day is treating you well so far," he said.

"Oh Tiny, this is Shatzie, she just came over from Germany and is going to be living here with us now. Shatzie, this is Tiny."

The little girl looked up at the mountain of a man, all of 6'8" and 270 pounds, and just stared. Tiny leaned down and took a small hand into his huge paw, gave it a little shake, and said, "Nice to meet you, Shatzie."

With a slight quiver in her voice Shatzie stammered, "You can't be Tiny. You are so big. You must be a giant. Are you a giant? Why are you called Tiny?"

The mountain knelt down on one knee and with a twinkle in his eye and a glance at the adults seemingly anxious to hear his answer and still holding her hand, he explained, "Yes, I am a giant. But you see, most giants are much taller than me," holding a hand well above his head, "and much wider," stretching his arms out from his shoulder. "But I am not tall or wide. I am small giant so that's why they call me Tiny."

"But giants are mean and grumpy, not like you. Are you sure you're a giant?"

Tiny slowly rose to his feet, leaned over and spoke quietly. "You are right, most giants are mean and grumpy. But that's my father's side of the family. I take after my mother's side, quiet and gentle, like your mom and Dad, and your friend Natalie. We are all friendly and nice."

Shatzie thought for minute. "Tiny," she asked fervently, "can I be your friend?"

Like the kiss from God, Tiny leaned down and touched his lips to his new friend's golden hair. "Of course, my dear, I love new little friends like you! Thank you."

"But even giants must work, so back to work I go. Have a good breakfast," as the tiny giant made his way back to the kitchen.

Shatzie couldn't believe what had just happened. "Mommy, I have a giant friend," she happily explained to her mother. "None of my friends have a giant friend. Wait till I tell them!"

The adults around the table smiled at the childhood wonder that each of them had experienced years ago and they now witnessed and shared again. It was a beautiful feeling.

Breakfast arrived and was eaten with haste befitting those who had not eaten in a while. When all was done and the hunger pains extinguished, they sat back and relaxed, looking forward to the rest of the day.

"Shatzie," asked Natalie, "would you like to see the ocean?"

"You mean the one we flew over yesterday?"

"Yes, my dear, we can go take a walk along the beach and watch the waves and even get our feet wet. It'll be fun."

"Oh," said Sophie, "but she has her good shoes on. They well get ruined."

Smiling, Naralie reached into her purse and pulled out a tiny pair of red flip-flops. "That's what I bought these for. No worry now. We can get as wet as we want."

Sophie nodded in agreement.

"So, my little Shatzie, put these on and let's go explore the wonderful world of the ocean."

And with that, the two of them said goodbye, and holding hands, they went to explore a new world.

Chapter Forty-Nine

atalie carried Shatzie down the stairs to the walkway below Beach Bum's and set her down to walk. She took her little hand and started toward the beach with the child looking around at amazing new things.

A couple of yards toward the beach they passed between the two wooden benches arranged just before the end of the walkway and at the start of the sandy beach. Natalie stopped and sat down on one of the benches.

"Shatzie," she said, "let's leave our shoes here. We can pick them up on the way back after we rinse off our feet."

The young girl watched Natalie take off her sandals, tie them together and place them on the bench seat. She took off her newly acquired flip-flops and placed them next to Natalie's, looking up at her guide waiting for the next step.

With a "let's go," Natalie took the little hand and stepped onto the sand and into a new adventure. In a few moments, the two mounted the last sand dune and stared at the magnificent blue water of the Atlantic Ocean, its crawling watery fingers lapping at the sand, then disappearing back to where they came from. For the first time observer, it was unreal.

"Natalie, is that the ocean? It seems different."

Natalie continued looking straight ahead. "It is different than the ocean you see from a plane. This is the edge of the ocean. It stops here, at the shore, and only gives a hint of what we can't see. It's like a road. We can see the beginning and perhaps a little more. but we can't see the last of it until we get there. That is why the ocean is so mysterious. We just don't know much about it. Come on, let's take a walk."

The two strolled toward the water's edge, the sand rubbing against their bare feet as it crept between their toes. Shatzie had never walked on sand before, it was a new sensation, and a little bit uncomfortable. They moved closer and closer to the water's edge, finally feeling the cold tiny waves as they washed away the sand.

And the sand was gone, no longer crumpled pieces of something, instead a smooth and flat surface. "Natalie, where did the sand go?"

"Oh, it's still here, just smoothed out by the water. You can see the difference in color and feel. It's the same stuff but changed by the waves."

"But where does the sand come from? I don't see any trucks or wagons. How does it get here?"

Natalie smiled at the questions the little one asked. It was refreshing to address them rather than those from work. Natalie thought for a minute.

"See those big rocks over there, those boulders? Well, this sand, all this sand, was once a part of a boulder. Years and years of pounding and scraping by the ocean, by the waves, slowly scratched away the boulders and made tiny pieces of rock. More and more scraping and washing by the ocean turned the rocks into smaller pieces and after a while, into sand. So, time and water made the sand."

"But what about that rock?" pointing to a rocky outcropping about two feet high sticking up from the sand. "It's stuck in the middle of the sand. Is the water going to wash it away too?"

"Well, maybe." said Natalie. "You see, some rocks are stronger than others. They can last a long time. In fact, if used right, if cared for, they can last hundreds, even thousands of years. Castles built thousands of years ago still stand. The pyramids-built thousands of years ago still stand. Even ideas, built upon a rock, they still stand."

"Can I go stand on the rock?" said Shatzie. "I want to be around for a long time."

Natalie smiled and led her over to the rock. Holding one hand, she helped the little girl to the top of the rock, steadying her till she gained her balance, then stepped back.

Shatzie stretched out her arms as though flying like a bird and slowly turned in a small circle till she arrived back at the starting point. "I could see everything," she said. "It was wonderful and fun. Can we stay for a while?"

Natalie reluctantly shook her head. "No more today. People are waiting for us back at the restaurant. But there are plenty of more days ahead and we can do it again. Would you like that?"

"Yes," said the little bird. "I would like that."

With that, Natalie grabbed her little hand, helped her down from the pedestal she had mounted and started walking back to the restaurant, stopping only to wash off the sand and grab their shoes.

"Mommy! Mommy! I stood on the rock on the beach. It was high and I could see everything," Shatzie said excitedly as she ran to her mother. "Natalie said we could go back again so I could see it all over again!"

Natalie caught up to the little girl and sat down at the table. Sophie hugged her daughter while John, Stick, and Chris watched the scene unfold.

"I hope she wasn't too much of a bother," said Sophie. "She can be quite a handful."

"Not at all," responded Natalie. "If her grandmother, oops, her Oma can handle her, I am sure hoping that I can also."

Shatzie looked sadly at Natalie. "I don't have my Oma anymore. She went away."

"Away?" asked Natalie.

"Yes, Mommy said she went to visit God and would probably stay there for a long time. But I can see her when I go visit God too. It will be good to talk to her again."

Natalie glanced over at Sophie with a questioning look. Sophie nodded and mouthed the word "died" and continued commenting out loud. "Yes, Oma went to visit God and Tomas is retiring and selling the Gasthaus to one of the cousins. Add those things to John's work, well, that's why we decided to come to America. Somewhat of a fresh start."

Silence fell over the table until Chris stood up and reminded Natalie of the things they had to do that day. And with that, the spell was broken, and all got ready to leave. With good-byes, hugs, and kisses, they gathered their belongings and headed for the exits. Stopping abruptly, Natalie turned to John. "John, when you come into work on Monday, stop by the office before seeing Dick. I want to discuss something with you."

John acknowledged the request, and they all went their separate ways.

Chapter Fifty

Monday morning, Natalie shut the car door with a slam to ensure it was staying shut. It was about time to get a newer one, she thought, as with all things, time runs out. She entered the front door of the office building and slowly walked up the steps to the lobby and her office.

Reaching the top, she was surprised to see John sitting there talking with Margaret, the two of them staring at her as she conquered the last steps.

"John, what are you doing here so early. I didn't expect you so soon."

John stood up from his chair. "I came in a couple of hours early to chat with the night crew to get a handle on things before talking with you and Dick and starting the day. But," he said glancing at his watch which read 8:15, "I didn't realize you were only working half a day." A smile slowly creeped across his face.

With a scow on her face, Natalie deflected the snide comment and turned to Margaret asking, "Did Janet leave anything for me over the weekend? She mentioned she might."

Margaret nodded and reached into her private desk drawer, retrieving a sealed envelope and handed it to Natalie. "She said to give it to no one but you."

"Thanks," said Natalie as she took the envelope and headed to her office. Turning back, she looked at John and said, "Oh, you might as well come in also," with a look of feigned disdain on her face. "And shut the door."

John got up and with a smile on his face and a thumbs up, he looked at Margaret and proceeded to march into Natalie's office. With a flick of the wrist, the door was shut.

"How was the rest of your weekend, John? Do anything special?"

"Nothing really. Got settled in the cabin, worked through the time change, and of course, watching Shatzie is always a handful. But it was good. Have to tell you, though, whatever you and Shatzie did or talked about during your walk really stuck with her. That's pretty much all she could talk about, you and the darn rock! It was like she owned it and wanted to go back and see it again and again and again. She constantly asked, 'When are we going to see Natalie again? I want to talk to her,' etc. To tell the truth, it eventually got tiring."

Natalie laughed. "Yea, we had a fun time on the beach. Little kids are like a blank slate, whatever you say to them stays with them till you erase it so you must be careful with that. But she listens well, understands most of what you say, and responds in a pretty adult way. She's going to be a lovely and smart young lady."

"But that's not what I want to talk to you about, John. Read this while I make some coffee, we're going to need it before we are done. One cup or two?"

John looked a little confused, but opening the envelope and taking out the contents, he replied, "Two, please."

The next several minutes were quiet as Natalie worked her magic with the coffee pot and John read the document from the envelope. When the coffee was done, Natalie poured two cups and set them down on the table and sat across from John, who had just finished reading.

Looking up, he said, "That is quite a job description. Have you talked to Superman about this job yet?"

Natalie laughed. "Not yet, thought I would pass it by you first."

John leaned back in his chair. "Well, think you have covered all the bases here, from Operations to Quality Assurance, and everything in-between. I don't know anyone who could meet all those requirements. Where did you get them from?"

"Janet put it together, after discussions with several of the Directors and me. I thought it was a pretty good description of what I'm looking for, but you are right, finding the candidate who fits all that would usually be a challenge."

"Yea, good luck with that. I'll think about it and see if anyone comes to mind. If so, I'll let you know," said John starting to get up.

"John, I think I found him."

John stopped in his tracks. Confusion reigned around him as he tried to comprehend what Natalie was saying. Nothing made sense.

"What?"

"I think I found him," repeated Natalie.

"What? Who?"

"John," said Natalie quietly, "it's you."

John stood like a statue, his world swirling around him. "Me? What do you mean 'me'?"

"It's you, John. This job description was written for you. No one else can match it. It was intended for you."

"I don't understand," said John, a confused look on his face. "Why?"

Natalie longed to explain. "Time has moved on, John. I am no longer the young woman who was thrust into the position that I have held for many years. Holding on to it has been wonderful but has also been a challenge. This latest bout with the Board of Directors has reminded me that change is inevitable, it is going to happen. But being the person I am, I want it to happen on my terms, the way I want it, not the way someone else wants it. This is my company, started by my father, given to me after his death and through my struggles to establish my ownership, and I don't want to give it up.

"When we first met, I thought there was something special about you. That's why I made sure you got an application for the intern program. I wanted you in my company because I thought you would make better - and I still do.

"Later this week the Board of Directors is meeting and on the agenda is a proposition that the position of Vice President of Condor be established. I have the votes for that to happen, so that is not the issue. The issue is who will have that position. Hence the job description, hence it being written for you, and hence, the job, if you want it is going to be yours. It is up to you."

With a look of protest John responded, "But I don't know anything about running a company like this. I have no experience in doing that. Yes, I have experience in the areas mentioned in the job description, but there are other areas that are totally foreign to me."

"John," laughed Natalie. "That is what I admire about you and why I want you as Vice President. You not only know your strengths, but also your weaknesses. Few people can see that. And you are right, there are areas in which you are a novice. I'm thinking specifically of Human Resources and Marketing. But think of yourself as being in the intern program again and I am your mentor. It is I that will lead you in learning those areas, it is I that will teach you, and it is I that will decide when you are ready to assume the leadership of this company and continue the traditions and culture established over the many years. When the time comes, John, you will be ready."

Like a frozen puppet, John stood there with his mouth wide open, listening to Natalie explain her life's goals. It was a lot to take in, in such a short period of time. "I don't know," he said. "I just don't know."

Natalie had heard that before sitting in a cemetery and completely understood the feeling. "I understand John, this comes as a surprise to you. Take some time to think about it. The Board meeting is Thursday, and the position is going to be established. The publication of the open position will not take place until the following week, so you have time. Talk it over with Sophie, think about Shatzie, and decide. No matter what you decide, you will always have a home here at Condor, don't forget that."

"Now, finish your coffee and go talk to Dick. He is a trusted friend and we talked about this conversation. Only he, Janet, Margaret, and I are aware, so please don't discuss it with anyone else other than your family to include Stick. Take your time, think clearly, and please don't bang the wall on the way out. I just had the office painted."

Natalie stood and watched John as he walked out as though carrying the weight of the world.

"God bless him," she thought.

Chapter Fifty-One

John and Sophie sat on the chairs on Stick's porch enjoying the afternoon sun and the sound of the waves down the walk. There is something soothing about the sound of water, be it at the ocean's edge, a fountain in a park, or the splashing of water as it flows over normally dry rocks in the desert.

It just seems to carry one away from the cares of the world to the serene atmosphere of self-indulgence, taking care of oneself. That is needed at times.

Natalie and Shatzie sat on the steps of the porch looking at books, reading little snippets and commenting on their meanings. It was an exercise both of them enjoyed, Shatzie for learning and Natalie for teaching and, at times, learning also. Laughing and giggling was a big part of the enjoyment and had been ever since they met.

The last three months had been one new experience after another, each learning more and more about each other. Shatzie soaked up all Natalie had to offer like a huge sponge, and Natalie thoroughly enjoyed opening new venues for her to enjoy. From music to art to architecture and even to business, and of course flying. It was all new to Shatzie and freely and cheerfully given by Natalie.

With a wave of his hand and a cherry "Hi folks," Stick rounded the corner and approached the four of them sitting on the porch. His walking stick tapped steadily as he came closer and with a sigh of relief, plumped himself down on the steps alongside Shatzie.

"What's you doing?"

"Natalie's teaching me more stuff. I never knew there was so much to learn."

The adults laughed with the knowledge that the learning part had just begun and there was much more ahead.

"John," said Stick. "How is the new Vice President job coming? Gotten off the cloud yet?" he laughed.

John's eyes met Natalie's as she waited for his answer.

"Well, it's coming along. My new boss is really a taskmaster, never done showing me new things and telling me how to do things. Kind of annoying at times. I'm thinking of quitting."

Natalie's back stiffened and she stared at him, growling under her breath.

John laughed. "Just kidding," he said, "it's actually coming along well. Quite a challenge, never a dull moment, and I'm learning a lot about the business that I never knew existed. I should have it down pat in, oh I don't know, about twenty or thirty years."

"Nah, Stick," said Natalie. "He's doing fine. We're getting there."

Shatzie, listening the whole time, asked Natalie, "Are you teaching Daddy too?"

Natalie looked down at the little girl. "Yes dear. Different things of course. We never stop learning, even when we grow up, which some of us need to do," she said looking up at John.

Sophie laughed and slapped John on the shoulder. "See, I told you to grow up. You can't buy an airplane, as much as you would like to."

"Why not, Dad has one."

Shatzie's head swiveled from John to Stick to John to Stick and back and forth like a clock pendulum.

"Grandpa, you have an airplane?"

In a flash, the conversation had changed.

***

The two-car convoy turned off the main highway onto the macadam road snaking across the open field toward the worn-out shack once bustling with activity.

Stick, riding in the lead car with John driving and Sophie in the back seat, swung his head around, looking as his past swept by with each rotation of the wheels, bring back memories bitter and sweet, but memories, nevertheless.

Behind them, Chris followed at a comfortable distance, also remembering his attendance at a ceremony honoring Stick. Natalie sat in the front and Shatzie rode in the back, sitting on the edge of the seat as if entering a new world.

"Natalie," asked Shatzie, "have you been here before?"

"Many times. This is a special place for me."

"Why?"

"Well," Natalie hesitated, "because my Daddy's plane is here too."

170

"Your Daddy had a plane too?" the little girl asked excitedly.

"Yes," said Natalie. "He flew his plane into Germany right after the war. That's when he met my mother."

"Your mother was German?"

"Yes, dear. She was German. But she came to the United States when her father thought there was going to be another war and he didn't want to be in Germany when it started."

"So, your whole family moved to America then?"

"No, just my grandfather and my mother. I was not yet born. My Papa and Oma had already gone to see God," she replied using the term Sophie had taught her daughter. "So, we went by ourselves."

"So, you had no Oma?"

"No," said Natalie, unaware of where this was leading.

Quiet, a natural consequence of thinking, filled the air as each occupant recalled their own past.

"I don't have an Oma either," said the young person in the back seat, sadly, as tiny tears filled her eyes. "I miss my Oma."

Natalie turned around to Shatzie. "I know, they are special people, especially to little ones, like you, who are just growing up. They are a wonderful source of information, of history, of life before we were born, or trials and tribulations they went through to get where they are. They are like the books you and I read, but better, because we can talk to them, ask questions, and get answers. They are a special part of life. And an important part of life."

Like a bolt of lightning out of the sky, slicing through all the flak in human lives, parting the curtains that prevent us from seeing reality, and throwing open the door of who we really are, the question came.

"Natalie, will you be my Oma?"

Chris looked over at Natalie who had a blank look on her face, as if the simple question had just released a hidden desire, a desire so deep that even she hadn't thought of it.

Years raced by in a few seconds, thoughts of yesteryear, remembrances of happy times with grandparents and sad times when they went to see God. But it was the happy times that seemed to overwhelm the bad, and it was the thought of bringing happy times to one little girl that shoved everything else out of the way.

"Shatzie, I'm not sure I can be an Oma. Oma's are special people who provide a respite, sorry, who provide a place to go to get away from things. Kind of like a little cave with a cozy blanket and a soft pillow to rest on. And they listen. The listen to dreams and goals, and 'I wanna do this' and 'I wanna be that when I grow up.' They don't ever say 'no,' At worst they say 'maybe' but they always leave the door open for you to achieve your best. They truly are God's gift."

"I don't know if I can do that."

Shatzie listened quietly, taking it all in. And with the unbridled wisdom of Soloman, the heartfelt caring of a Nightingale, and the softness of the most honest angel, she replied, "You already are."

The shroud was lifted from the doubt as the realization came forth that she was already doing it, and without knowing it, had begun a new chapter in her life. And with the tiniest of fears slipping away, and the ascension of will, hope, and belief in the happiness of children, Natalie replied, "Shatzie, Ingrid, I will try."

The two cars pulled up to the dirty hanger doors shut for a long time, waiting to be opened and to display their treasures inside. The inhabitants got out of the cars and Stick reached for his keys and walked to the pedestrian door.

He opened the door and disappeared only to reappear between the large hanger doors as they slowly and not so quietly slid open. The others waited a minute to ensure the doors would remain open, then reverently entered the past.

Natalie and Shatzie entered first, kicking up dust that had been there for a long time. Chris and John followed with Sophie not far behind, but bringing up the rear, not sure of what was inside.

 Stick reached for a switch and the large, bright overhead lights brought to live the bodies of the two planes; planes that instantly transformed the dingy hanger into a glorious monument of the trials and tribulations that bought them there.

Grandmom and granddaughter walked over to the DC-7, touching the smoothness of its wings before feeling the iron skin of its body. With a slight tug, the stairs leading into the fuselage slowly unfolded and settled on the hanger floor, scattering the dust as though laying a welcome sign.

"Would you like to go inside?" asked Natalie.

Hesitantly, the little girl responded, "Will you go with me?"

"Absolutely, in fact I'll go first," Natalie said as he gingerly climbed the stairs.

In a flash, Shatzie followed, eyes opened to the sights to be seen. Though it was only ten minutes, it seemed like hours till they exited the plane. Stick stood ready, and led them over to his biplane, still covered in bright red paint, "Candy Man" announcing to the world its stated mission. Stick reached into his side pocket and pulled out a Hershey Candy Kiss and offered it to Shatzie.

She looked, not at her parents, but at her newly found grandmother for approval. All three laughed and the young girl gobbled the chocolate down. Chris, who had been standing all this time and watching the proceedings, reached into his pocket and brought out a whole bag of candy.

He offered them around saying, "Never know when these are going to come in handy."

Natalie smiled and gave him a peck on the cheek, with a look that said, "More later."

Shatzie laughed and giggled, clasping her hands over her mouth.

They spent about another hour looking at the planes, sitting in the pilot's seat, imagining them flying among the clouds. Eventually it was time to go. Natalie grabbed Shatzie and started toward the door, the others following. Numerous thoughts had been going through her mind, brought on by the memories returned by the planes and by the discussion with Shatzie.

Turning round before reaching the hanger door, Natalie called for John to come with them. When he caught up with the two, Natalie pulled a keychain from her purse and handed it to John. "Here," she said, "don't let the place burn down."

John looked at the keychain and recognized it as the keys to the Condor office building. He stared at the keys and almost yelled at Natalie, "What are you doing?"

"They're yours now, John. I'll submit my resignation next week and the Board will anoint you with the new title. Take good care of the old gal, you both deserve each other."

Natalie turned and walked away holding Shatzie's hand. John, trying to stall, said, "Wait this can't be the end of an era."

Natalie turned and looked at him. She bent down and whispered something in Shatzie's ear.

With a slight turn to face her dad directly, the little girl repeated what her grandmom had said. "Dad, Oma says to tell you,

"There are no Endings
Only New Beginnings."

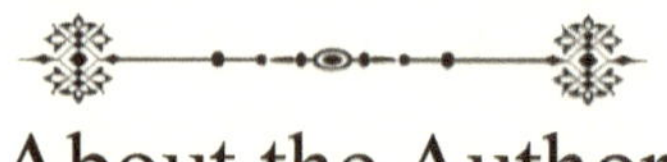

About the Author

Carl Messinger is a decorated Vietnam veteran who suffered through a C- freshman English class taught by a Pulitzer Prize winning professor which turned off his writing aspirations till much later in life. However, years later living in Germany provided him numerous opportunities to share his adventures and he began writing travel articles with the thought of "painting with words." The acceptance of several of these articles fueled the fire and intensified the desire to write.

Returning from Germany and with an amateur acting career, he settled in the Philadelphia area and combined his knowledge of the theater with writing and began writing theater reviews for a local newspaper. Later moving to the Washington D.C. he continued his coverage of professional theaters including the famed Folger's Theater known for its Shakespeare productions.

Real-life job opportunities moved him to Arizona where a chance discussion with a friend resulted in Tent City: An Arizona Tragedy, currently available on Amazon.

Endless Beginnings is the third and final book of a three-part series entitled The Pilot's Daughter. Only the future knows what lies ahead.

www.ingramcontent.com/pod-product-compliance
Lightning Source LLC
Chambersburg PA
CBHW031308160726
47993CB00001B/340